What others are saying about

Wooing CUPID

"Funny, touching, and very entertaining!"
—Rusty Allen, Amazon reviewer

"I was captivated... a feel good love story."
—reader, Amazon reviewer

"Susan Lohrer has a winner with this new series."
—Sunshine, Amazon reviewer

"Laced with fun and interspersed with such humour... a lighthearted read... where real life and fantasy collide."
— Lizzi McHappy, Amazon UK reviewer

Other Books by Susan Lohrer

Rocky Road (contemporary romance)

Over the Edge (contemporary romance)

Eagle Magus (fantasy romance, book 1 of Magus series)

Coming soon:

The Harrington series (small-town contemporary romance)

Wooing Bacchus (contemporary fantasy romance; book 2 of
the Wooing the Gods series)

Wooing Mercury (contemporary fantasy romance; book 3 of
the Wooing the Gods series)

Wolf Magus (fantasy romance; book 2 of Magus series)

Last Magus (fantasy romance; book 3 of Magus series)

Wooing
CUPID

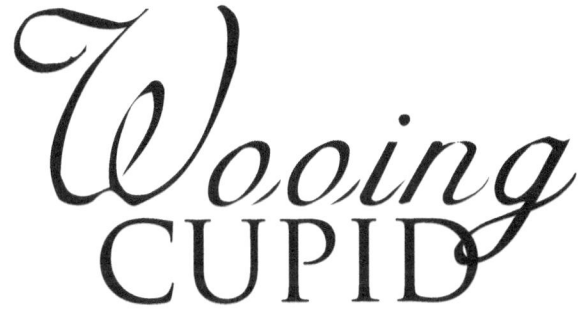

Wooing CUPID

BY

SUSAN LOHRER

STARSONG PUBLISHING

ISBN 978-0-9868665-5-5

WOOING CUPID

Cover art by Susan Lohrer.

Model photo by Zigf.

www.StarsongPublishing.com

Printed in the United States of America.

Acknowledgments

If not for the superhuman patience and understanding of my dear husband and our two teens who still live at home—the poor things ate so many burned/undercooked dinners that often were lacking key ingredients because my head was in the story—this book never would have been written.

My street team, affectionately nicknamed my ground crew by my mom, is a group of indefatigable ladies who help create a buzz about my books. If not for them, nobody would have known about *Wooing Cupid*.

And a very special thank-you to Angel, who has a sharp eye for typos.

Dear Reader,

If you're like me (I hope you are, at least a little bit), you read in more than one genre. WOOING CUPID is a bridge between my contemporary romance and my fantasy. It's... contemporary fantasy romance, and you'll find a similar sense of humor and the same theme of family and friends that you loved in ROCKY ROAD and OVER THE EDGE, with a good dose of the magic you loved in EAGLE MAGUS.

There's a deliberate bit of artistic license taken with Vittorio Fulminare's choice of Italian cuisine in WOOING CUPID. I fully realize fish is a popular food in Italy, but I simply couldn't bring myself to believe fish is a romantic thing to eat, authentic or not. So Vittorio and Val end up eating pasta (probably with a lot of yummy cheese).

And of course, Cupid is traditionally a male god. Hm... not anymore.

I do hope you like this little story. I always love to hear from my readers, and you can e-mail me at susan@susanlohrer.com.

From my heart to yours,

Susan

P. S.: Get e-mail alerts (once or twice a year) about my new releases by signing up for my newsletter at www.susanlohrer.com/p/newsletter.html.

one

AFRIGID FEBRUARY WIND blasted the streets of Cupid's Hollow and hurried Valentine Arciere's steps as she and her grandmother arrived at Valentine Sports. Val unlocked the door. The buildings on either side of the store stood dark and empty, snowdrifts banked against their entrances. The desolation painted a grim contrast to the bright, bold posters that decorated every window on Main Street advertising the Valentine's Day Gala just two weeks from today.

She sucked in a deep breath and raised her chin as she pushed open the door, the brass bell tinkling overhead to announce her arrival. She'd hung that bell the day she signed her name on the deed beside Gram's. The bell's tone sang out the sound of hope, the sound of independence, every time the shop door opened. Which, lately, wasn't often enough.

She flicked on the light and saw a crudely lettered warning lying on the floor. Again. She stooped to pick it up before her grandmother, who was right behind her, could see the lettering. But Gram plucked the paper from her hand. The wrinkles around her mouth puckered.

"Sell now or you'll be sorry?" Gram blinked up at her, her eyes magnified comically behind her new bifocals. The paper rustled in her hands. "Valentine, what is this? Who's threatening us?"

"It's nothing, Gram." Val plucked up the paper, wadded it, and tossed it into the recycling bin behind the counter.

"Maybe we should lease out the store," Gram whispered. "I could retire. You could travel. It might not be such a bad thing to find out what else life might hold in store for you." If Gram believed that, why did she sound so devastated—like she'd given up? But Val noticed Gram hadn't gone so far as to suggest actually selling out. The family business still meant everything to her, just as it did to Val.

On the wall above the counter, a photo of her parents showed them laughing in the sun on their sailboat, *Salacia*, somewhere in the Mediterranean. They'd e-mailed the shot a day before a storm sank their boat. That photo, and the sports shop her parents had named after her, were all she had of them. All Gram had of her daughter.

"This store *is* my life, Gram. I don't need to travel to find out what's important to me."

Gram's mouth bunched in a soft smile. "I know, little Valentine. Your mom and dad would be very proud of what you've done with the store—and with your life—and so am I. I'll be in the back if you need me, making a paper airplane from that offer we got from Jupitropolis."

Val laughed. But after Gram trundled into the office at the back of the store, she braced her hands on the glass top of the counter and breathed deeply. Gram had never said anything about retiring before, so this was the first time Val had thought of her grandmother as anything but a sprightly older lady, the one person in her life who would always be there.

But Gram *was* getting older.

Every business on Main Street except theirs had eventually sold out when Jupitropolis offered sums that to the small-town shop owners seemed outrageously generous. Jupiter's megastore was offering jobs, pensions, even a modest health care plan. When the first letter arrived offering to buy the sports shop, standing her ground had seemed like the only sensible idea. It was a matter of principle. A principle, it seemed, that only Valentine believed in anymore.

If she gave in, Cupid's Hollow would become just one more community powered by the gaudy plastic heart of Jupitropolis.

If she refused to sell, she would be singlehandedly responsible for destroying the economy of Cupid's Hollow.

She raised her head and blinked away the moisture that blurred the image of her parents, wishing she could somehow break through the barriers of time. "Mom, what should I do?"

The bell tinkled softly, and her first customer of the day walked into the store.

The customer browsed, and Val watched him from the corner of her eye as she rearranged a display of ski gloves that didn't need rearranging. The bottom edge of his leather jacket reached the knees of his expensively cut pants, and he wore a black dress shirt that draped like silk over the muscular contours of his chest. Judging by his clothing, this guy definitely wasn't a local.

The air felt thicker somehow, as though she were in a greenhouse. He picked up a basketball and spun it on his finger for a few seconds then stilled it and turned to face her. He had the darkest, most expressive eyes she'd ever seen, and the intensity of his gaze made her feel as though he were probing her innermost secrets.

She managed to break their eye contact, but then a couple of seconds later she found herself not just staring at him but ogling him. His hair was long and dark and he wore it loose. What would it feel like against her face? Her shoulders?

"Can I help you find something?" She'd like to help him find one thing in particular—her.

"I think you can." One side of his mouth curved upward invitingly.

She bit her lip, and his breath hitched.

Her belly tightened. She heard a soft gasp and realized it had come from her.

Squeezing her eyes shut, she whirled to put her back to him. What in the world was wrong with her? She wasn't the kind of woman who threw herself at men. She barely even dated. And here she was practically panting at a perfect stranger's feet. *Perfect* being the operative word. She shook her head to try to jar some sense into it. For all she knew, this guy was from Jupitropolis. He was probably the one who'd stuffed the threatening note under her door and was here to gauge her reaction. Or maybe the company had sent a goon to make good on the threat that she'd be sorry she hadn't sold.

She took a long, slow breath and blew it out, firmly reminded herself that this was *her* store and it was going to stay her store, and turned to face him again.

This time he smiled at her, and her legs might as well have been loose bowstrings. While the energy radiating from her stranger's taut body was a tightly strung bow. *Breathe, Val, and for heaven's sake, he's not your stranger. He's not your anything.* "What is it that you're looking for today?"

"Not what." He set down the ball. "Whom."

How could good grammar be so bone-meltingly swoon worthy? "Okay, so whom are you looking for?"

Should she have said *for whom are you looking*?

"You."

Her pulse rushed in her head like the rhythm of the sea. Magnificent, vast, capable of consuming a person without so much as a ripple to mark the passing. Just like Jupitropolis was trying to do to Cupid's Hollow. To her business. To her. She shook her head. "I'm not for sale."

"Everyone's for sale." He flashed a grin that made her thighs tingle despite his arrogance. "But that's not quite what

I was asking. I'm thinking of moving to your little town, and what better way to explore it than to meet someone who lives here? And clearly I've forgotten my manners." He approached the counter that was the only barrier between them and held out his hand to her. "My name is Vittorio Fulminare, and I would be most honored if you would accompany me to the Valentine's Day Gala."

Feeling like she was committing an act of insanity she could never undo, like jumping from a plane or plunging into the depths of the sea, she placed her hand in his.

"I'd love to," she breathed. Had she really just said that?

He smiled, and his fingers closed around hers, warm despite the fact that he'd just come in from the bluster of February. He lifted her hand to his mouth and brushed a kiss over her knuckles, raising his eyes to meet hers once more. The caress of his lips against her skin made her insides tremble.

Vittorio. Even his name sent delicious tremors through her. Somewhere she found the will to remove her hand from his and say something less inane than the mushy romantic sentiments swirling through her brain.

"So... no one sent you to intimidate me into selling the store?" Heat crawled up her chest and into her neck. Maybe she shouldn't have attacked him like that. Maybe he really wasn't from Jupitropolis.

He gave her a heavy-lidded stare, the kind of stare a man saved for his lover. "Nobody sends me anywhere."

She believed him. The man was like a force of nature. The type of man who did whatever he damn well pleased. And if she kept gawking at him like this, he was going to think she wanted him to do more than just kiss her hand.

Well, didn't she?

No! No, she did not.

Maybe a little.

He smiled slowly as though he knew exactly what she was thinking.

Good thing he didn't, or they'd be making out right now between the Atomics and the Dynastars.

She was never going to be able to sell skis again without that image in her mind. Clearing her throat, she tapped a finger on the petition, taped prominently to the front edge of the sales counter. "If you're not from Jupitropolis, you might be interested in signing this."

He scanned the petition. "You're fighting such a powerful company? Do you really think you have a chance?"

"Of course I do. As long as my store stands, they can't build, and Cupid's Hollow keeps its heart and soul. Here's a pen." She pushed it across the counter.

He flipped the pen over in his hand then set it down without adding his signature. "Why would you do that? Doesn't Jupitropolis provide good jobs?"

"Big corporations like that chew up small towns and spit them out. They're just in it for the money. They don't care that they crush the small business owners or teach the youth that the only value that matters is the almighty dollar." But look who she was talking to. Or whom. His clothes probably cost what she earned in a month. He couldn't understand what she was talking about even if he tried.

So why did she want to crawl across the counter and kiss him until his eyes crossed?

A sound of movement from the back of the store re-minded her that the door to the office was ajar and Gram was back there, overhearing every word of their exchange. The thought bolstered her will to control her crazy attraction to this man she'd met only moments before. She had a busi-ness to run—her hometown to protect from the jaws of big business—and she didn't have the time or the inclination to get into any kind of entanglement with a man, let alone one who could make her forget about everything but him just by being in the room.

Okay, so she had the inclination. But that didn't mean she was going to act on it. Besides, he hadn't signed her petition. She would never get involved with a man who didn't share her values.

His refusal should be merely annoying, but instead it hurt. No way was she going to be his little tour guide.

Then the solution to that particular problem occurred to her. She smiled in what she hoped was a disinterested manner despite the objectionably romantic thoughts coursing through her head, and she jotted a name and phone number on a Post-It note. "I know the perfect person to show you around town."

Deb, her best friend, regularly bemoaned the fact that there were no good men on the dating scene in Cupid's Hollow, and this guy was Deb's idea of Mr. Perfect. Getting the two of them together would be doing everyone a favor. And if Deb and Vittorio hit it off, that automatically put him off limits to Val. Problem solved.

A faint *twang* made her turn her head to the back of the store. The office door clicked shut—she hoped Gram wasn't about to go on eBay with the store credit card again, after the talk they'd had about that the other day.

She felt a stinging sensation on her left shoulder and brushed her hand across it. A glittering miniature arrow the length of her baby fingernail came free in her hand.

What was Gram up to now? Some kind of Valentine's Day promotion she'd forgotten to tell Val about? Whatever it was, she had to stop Gram before she started shooting tiny darts at their customers.

The stinging faded to a slight numbness, and she dropped the miniature arrow into her pocket. She pressed Deb's phone number into Vittorio's hand.

The moment she touched him, a jolt of electricity zapped between them. The lights dimmed for a second. She jerked back, cradling her hand, and glared at him. "Really hilarious, buddy." Ouch. He hadn't struck her as the kind of guy to play lame practical jokes.

He shrugged and held up his palms, looking ever so slightly guilty. She didn't see one of those hand buzzers. Only the bright yellow note she'd given him, clinging to the swell of muscle at the base of his thumb. Maybe what she'd felt was just his electric personality. Or maybe he was an expert at sleight of hand.

The burst of annoyance faded as soon as it had come. After all, it wasn't like he could voluntarily summon an electric current. If anything, she must have some kind of wiring problem and was lucky she'd gotten off with just a shock.

His pupils dilated till his eyes were almost completely black. His tongue traced a line between his teeth, and he braced both hands on the counter. Their faces were so close, she could smell his aftershave, fresh and sharp and clean as the Mediterranean air her parents had described in their e-mails. His breath caressed her mouth. "You felt that, yes?"

Would he taste as good as he smelled?

"Nope." She pulled away to prevent herself from accidentally kissing those firm-looking lips. "I didn't feel a thing."

Except the thing she was feeling made her want to sink her fingers into his hair and lock their mouths together until they both had to come up for air. Something was definitely, thoroughly wrong with her.

He peeled the Post-It off his palm and pressed it onto the counter with his thumb. "I won't be needing this."

"Okay. I guess I'll see you around." They were the most painful words she'd uttered.

"Tonight. When I pick you up for dinner."

She blinked. No. No-no-no-no—not only had he refused Deb's phone number, he was trying to make plans with *her*? She was *so* not interested. "Pardon me?"

"Is there a good Italian place in Cupid's Hollow?"

"Sure, it's a couple of blocks down, on the edge of town." He'd memorized the phone number, that was all. And she'd misheard him. He must've said he was picking *her* up, as in Deb. Not Val. She tried to feel relieved. Deb would go nuts over him, and Val would cheerfully bury her feelings as her best friend regaled her with tales of Vittorio's prowess as a boyfriend... a husband... a father. A bleak emptiness grew inside her.

"Good," he said with the bold masculine assurance Italian men seemed to take for granted. "I'll pick you up here at seven."

He strode out of her store before she could protest, the bell tinkling merrily.

Val wrapped her arms around herself, watching the confident set of his shoulders as he walked away. She still didn't know whether he was from Jupitropolis, and she'd was pretty sure she'd heard him right this time. Not only had she agreed to see him at the Valentine's Day Gala, she'd just agreed to go out to an intimate dinner with a guy who could well have been hired to take her business away from her.

The door to the office opened, and Gram puttered out, humming and pushing a carpet sweeper. Val dipped her hand into her pocket to retrieve the arrow. She felt around with her fingers, but the arrow was gone.

two

IN FRONT OF the hotel, Vittorio extricated himself from the tiny rental car that had been the only one available in Cupid's Hollow. Though he appreciated the finer things in life, he didn't mind roughing it from time to time. It was good for a descendant of the gods to live as mortals did. Spend too long isolated from the world and you grew out of touch—and then when you did need to interact with mortals, they could spot you a league away.

As he slid the key card into the door lock of his room, he reminded himself not to use words like *league*.

He needed to blend in so he could get close to this intriguing woman, Valentine Arciere, who stood between him and the erection of his next megastore. She'd actually had the audacity to ask him to sign her little petition. Him! And then she'd raised her defiant little chin and told me she wasn't for sale.

The memory of their brief encounter roused the image of her in his mind, fiery and yet soft, in his bed. He grunted and swung open the door.

His beer-bellied assistant, Randy, was lolling on one of the beds, madly pressing his thumbs on the hotel's video game controller while cartoon images flew across the TV screen. "So?" He drained a bottle of cheap beer without looking up from his game, then tossed the empty bottle onto the floor.

"She said yes." Vittorio closed the door and picked up the empty. He dropped it into the recycling bin. His assistant was a pig. Competent, but a pig.

"Figures. Here, don't let the dude with the wings die." Randy set down his drink, handed him the controller, and slid a folded bill from his wallet. He held it out to Vittorio then pulled it back. "Wait. What'd she say yes to?"

"Dinner."

"Huh. I figured you'd have banged her already."

"I figured you're such a randy little goat that you're the original reason the name Brandon was shortened to Randy." Vittorio reminded himself not to use words like *randy*.

"Look who's talking."

Indeed. Vittorio wasn't entirely comfortable with his feelings for Valentine Arciere, either. It wasn't like him to be this focused on one woman. He blasted a few video game demons and defeated the animated dark god without really looking at the screen then entered his own initials in the high score and tossed the controller onto the shelf below the TV. "Henceforth, you will refrain from making raunchy comments about Ms. Arciere."

"Jerk. I worked all day to beat that game." His assistant ceremoniously put the money back in his wallet before retrieving the remote. "You lost that bet on purpose, didn't you?"

Electricity sizzled from Vittorio and filled the room with the smell of hot electronics and the rumble of thunder. Light bulbs popped and went dark. The TV winked out. The bet—this one, anyway, had faded to insignificance the moment he'd laid his eyes on Valentine. She wasn't the kind of girl whose willingness to grant favors one bet upon. "She's a lady. I would dishonor the bet before I would dishonor her."

Randy dropped the smoking game controller. He flapped his hand, which was probably somewhat scorched; a hazard of working for a god. "You do know they're going to charge Jupitropolis for the damage, right?"

"It's not like I can't afford it. And Brandon—she is not like the others." Vittorio had always considered Brandon Allegri a friend regardless of the irreverent way he spoke in the presence of the direct line of the god Jupiter. But right now he could gladly strangle him. "You will not insult her again."

"Whatever you say, man." The other man stood. He held up his palms. "I get it. You like her. And I'll smooth things over with the hotel. Hey, it's my job. Right, boss?"

Vittorio could sense his assistant's underlying fear, and he expelled a hard breath. Randy wasn't just his employee, he was his friend. "It is more than that. She is different. Special. I… I apologize for—"

"Dude, don't break the illusion." Randy's voice wobbled through his bravado. "How'm I going to uphold my rep if it gets out that you've gone so soft you start apologizing because you sprouted *feelings* for a chick"—at Vittorio's scowl, he backed up a step—"I mean, a lady?"

Vittorio found he'd raised his fists. He relaxed his hands. "I need some food flown in from Father's *ristorante* by seven fifteen tonight." He gave the name and location of the local Italian restaurant. "And make sure there's good wine. Something of Bacchus's."

Let wily old Bacchus, the sot, wonder about that one. He reminded himself not to use words like *sot*.

"That's more like it." Randy pulled out his cell phone and made it happen.

Vittorio had come to this town to see for himself the woman who stood against Jupitropolis so he could understand how to defeat her, and he would. But now that he'd met her, a more urgent priority presented itself. She might think she was talking about business when she said she wasn't for sale, but he'd seen through the sassy words into the deep, primal knowledge in her eyes. She wasn't for sale at all. As sure as the blood of deity ran through his veins, Valentine Arciere already belonged to him.

Except there was the matter of the other wager he'd made. The one with Bacchus, with the feisty shop owner's soul at stake.

Midmorning passed without the usual lull between customers needing their skates sharpened, looking for good deals on mid-season ski passes, or—a first in Val's experience—visiting her sports shop to find a gift for the most romantic day of the year. Being the only store open on Main Street two weeks before Valentine's Day was great for business, but she hoped she'd be able to keep up with the frantic pace. When closing time came, half an hour later than usual, she turned over the sign, locked the door, and leaned against it to take a deep breath.

Instead of finding a nice blank thought, her mind zipped straight to the man she'd spoken to for just a few minutes this morning. All day she'd felt out of sorts, and now the little flutter in her stomach intensified until it felt like the wings of Cupid himself were swooping inside her.

Part of her wanted to believe Vittorio was simply a newcomer to town as he'd said, but she doubted that. Five minutes with him told her he was a man who got what he wanted, and he was accustomed to bending everyone else to his will. He didn't just *happen* to be anywhere. She replayed their conversation. He'd practically ordered her to go out to dinner with him. For an instant she'd felt like she had enough backbone to resist him. But then before she knew it, she'd agreed to the date as though she were a love-struck teenager.

She glanced at the clock on the wall over the counter. An hour and a half didn't seem like enough time to close out the till and then shower and get ready for a date she wasn't sure she wanted to go on. If she knew Vittorio's phone number, she'd call and cancel, but he hadn't given it to her. Even that made her feel as though he were exercising control over her. She supposed she could beg off when he showed up.

And then she realized she hadn't given him her number or home address either, so unless she met him here at the store at seven o'clock, he wouldn't be able to pick her up after all. The thought gave her a sense of having won a small battle, and she smirked to herself. But then she realized she'd have to decide whether she intended to show up. She closed her eyes and ground her teeth together. She'd decide later.

The only other shadow on her day had been the bizarre "shooting" incident. It had been a one-time thing—she hoped—but still, she had to talk to Gram about it. Zinging one's customers with miniature arrows would be a violation of heaven only knew how many laws and safety codes. Besides which, it was just plain wrong.

She checked all her pockets again for the tiny arrow, even feeling for holes. There were no holes, no arrow. But she'd *seen* that metallic flash, and the spot on her shoulder was still numb. She hadn't imagined it. She looked up at the photo of her parents on their sailboat and wished they were here to help her on days like today. But they weren't, so she plodded to the back of the store to join Gram in the office.

A couple of boxes were stacked against the back wall, their contents waiting to be put into inventory in the computer before being stocked. The shipping labels bore the eBay logo. Hopefully Gram had found a good deal. She'd ask later, because right discussing Gram's new foray into being a sniper was more urgent than her online shopping escapades.

Gram looked up and tapped the keyboard, but not before Val recognized the blue-and-white reflection in her new glasses. Facebook. Then it was back to the QuickBooks screen. Gram hovered her finger over the number pad. "Was that forty pairs of hockey skates or forty-one I heard?"

She'd never said anything to Gram about spending time online at work, just as she never minded when customers wandered back to the office to chat with Gram. Gram's outgoing personality had just as much to do with the success of Valentine Sports as Val's business sense did. Maybe more.

"We sharpened forty-one pairs," she said, and Gram updated the total in the computer. "Um, Gram?"

She moved the mouse and clicked, and the soft whir of the computer fell silent. "Yes?"

"Earlier today, just after we opened—"

"The little arrow." Gram propped her elbows on the desk, folded her hands under her chin, gazed candidly at Val. "Sweetie, we need to have a chat about that."

Val felt her mouth drop open. She sat on the edge of the desk. "Yes. We do."

"I haven't been the most diligent grandmother, I'm afraid."

"Of course you have. You've always been there for me. You've—"

"I neglected to tell you something about your heritage, Valentine." Gram's fingers twisted together tightly. "Something rather important."

Val could feel the muscles in her forehead bunching together. Had Gram received news about her parents? Anything regarding her parents, even the smallest particle of information, would be a gift. "Were Mom and Dad… were their bodies found?"

Gram shook her head. She rolled her chair back and came around the desk to enfold Val in a hug that almost took the ache away. Almost. Then she stood back, her hands warm and firm on Val's shoulders. "This goes much further back than one generation. Back to the time of the ancients. Valentine, we are descendants of the gods."

"Oh, Gram." She massaged her temples. She'd hidden the prescription bottle, but obviously not well enough. "You took another of those sleeping pills, didn't you?"

But Gram's solemn expression as she shook her head didn't fit with her previous chemically enhanced exploits. Moving deliberately and with good coordination, she opened the desk drawer and pulled out her shoulder bag. She rummaged inside it and produced an intricately crafted miniature crossbow. It was so small, it fit on her palm.

And it was loaded, a glittering golden bolt shaped like a tiny arrow ready to be loosed upon Gram's next unsuspecting victim.

Val sat still, silent, vaguely aware that the edge of the desk was poking uncomfortably into the back of her right thigh. She rubbed the numb spot on her shoulder. How did one respond when one's beloved Gram had suddenly and completely lost her marbles?

Gram picked up Val's hand and set the tiny bow on her palm. "Cupid's bow has belonged to our family for all time, passed from one guardian to the next. Now it belongs to you."

"Wow, gee, Gram. Thanks a bunch. I'll take good care of it." Carefully she removed the bolt. The only remotely positive aspect of this conversation was that Gram had willingly handed over the miniature weapon, and now Val wouldn't have to worry about having a bifocal-wearing septuagenarian sniper in the back of her store.

"This is no joking matter." Gram held up her finger, still dead serious. "A great responsibility has been conferred upon you."

"Sure, Gram." She tucked the tiny bow and arrow into her own purse. "I promise, I'm not taking this lightly. Let's go home, okay?"

With a beleaguered sigh, Gram fetched her parka from the coat rack and slid her arms into the sleeves. She yawned. Maybe she *had* taken a sleeping pill.

The business about Cupid's bow decided it. Val couldn't go out tonight, not with Gram hopped up on goof pills. She could come home to find the living room furniture rearranged with the sofa upside down again, or discover later that Gram had joined another online dating site. Or far, far worse—but she couldn't allow herself to think about that. She couldn't bear to think what it would be like to go through life without the only person in the world who loved her.

three

When Vittorio arrived at Valentine Sports, the windows were dark and the shop was locked up tight.

He frowned and checked the time on his Panerai. He was neither early nor late.

There was no bright yellow police tape nor any other indication that an unfortunate situation would have prevented her from being here at the appointed time.

Slowly, horrifyingly, it occurred to Vittorio that he may have been stood up. But no, she was a mortal woman smitten by just the hint of god powers mortals could sense. He'd seen *that* in her eyes this morning.

So it was impossible that she had slighted him that way. Still, she was mortal. And though mortals could seldom muster the willpower to deny a god, they were sometimes forgetful. He'd slipped her mind.

Another first. It almost stung.

No matter. Randy could dig up her contact information. He slapped his phone to his ear and spoke the command. It sent him to voice mail. He tried again. Same result.

Then, recalling his earlier slip when he'd destroyed the electronics in the hotel room, he realized his jolt of electricity must have bricked Randy's phone. It wouldn't be the first time—and by now the man really should know better than to purchase a device named after fruit.

Swearing, he tucked himself back into his conveyance

and sped back to the hotel, adjusting traffic lights as necessary along the way.

At the hotel he found an empty room with a note on the desk: "All details set. Taking the night off. R."

He set the paper back on the desk. Bacchus was behind this somehow. He had to be. The wine-addled excuse for a god thought he could win their wager for the mortal woman's soul simply by distracting Vittorio's right-hand man? Bacchus had delusions of grandeur, then.

Reminding himself not to use words like *addled*, he located and turned on every piece of electronics in the room, seeking one that would connect to the Internet. All were malfunctioning at best.

Finally he happened across the contents of the desk drawer. He slapped his forehead. Such a simple solution. He opened the phone book and paged through it until he found the entry for Valentine Arciere, complete with her street address.

Six minutes later he stood on the doorstep of a quaint house on the edge of town and pressed the button for the doorbell.

It took an eternity for her to open the door, but when she did, the wait was worth it. In jeans and a form-fitting T-shirt, with her pale blond hair damp and tousled around her shoulders, Valentine put to shame every woman he'd ever seen, mortals and goddesses alike.

Her eyebrows drew together, forming a delicate vertical crease between them that he wanted to smooth out with his lips. She opened her soft, inviting mouth.

"I can't go out with you." She stepped back and swung the door as though she meant to close it in his face.

No woman had ever behaved in such a fashion toward him. He was a descendant of the supreme ruler of the gods, and even those who didn't know that still *knew* it. He'd even had to fend off the amorous advances of a male friend or two, if they'd been in their cups. It came with the job.

He jammed his shoe in the way of the door. "Nonsense, I'll wait while you—"

In the instant between his picturing her in a state of dishabille while she chose an outfit and his finishing the sentence, the steel-encased door struck the instep of his foot. It took an instant for the impact to register in his brain. When it did, Vittorio sucked in a loud, hissing breath.

His ancestors had been battle-hardened warriors, well accustomed to physical assault. Their twenty-first-century progeny was accustomed to no such thing, and for the moment the only action he was capable of was to grasp the door frame and wheeze.

Eventually his senses began to return. He saw light first, in the form of a halo around Valentine's very feminine silhouette. A few seconds more and he could register color; the glittering green of her eyes.

Look how sweet she was with her crossed arms that drew his attention to her bosom.

Look how fearsome her glare was.

Drat.

He coughed. "My deepest apologies." *Stop sounding like you're from some other millennium, you fop.* "I apologize. You must allow me to start over."

She narrowed her eyes to slits as though she were contemplating ways to kill him.

By all the gods, she was the most enchanting creature he'd ever seen.

He tossed his dignity into the ether and held out his hand to her. "Please?"

The worlds stood still while he waited for her to decide whether to grace him with her presence this evening.

Finally her expression softened. She glanced over her

shoulder, back into the house, and then stepped out on the porch and closed the door. "I'm sorry. It's not that I don't want to. Now just isn't a good time for me. My grandmother had a… difficult day, and I don't want to leave her alone."

The droop of her pretty mouth as she spoke of her grandmother tugged at his heart in a way he hadn't expected it to. He caught her hand in his.

"You're lucky to have her in your life," he guessed.

She nodded. "I am. She's the only family I have. So you can understand, then?"

"Absolutely." And if he didn't, he ought to. The day he'd learned the truth about the deity in his veins, he'd left his village home in Tuscany and sought his own way in life, never looking back. So he knew all too well what it was like not to have family. "Does your grandmother like Italian food?"

He hadn't become the head of a worldwide conglomerate just because of his looks.

"What?" She tilted her head as though peering at him from a different angle would reveal his thoughts to her.

So disingenuous. So utterly unaware of etiquette. So unlike any woman he'd ever been with. His heart beat a thunderous tattoo that filled his entire body.

"Bruschetta," he said, keeping his voice level only with much difficulty. "Manicotti. Linguine." He mimed twisting noodles against a spoon and putting them in his mouth, then closed his eyes and brought his fingers to his mouth and away in the universally recognized gesture of an Italian gustatory delight, suspecting he looked the fool but willing to risk it for the possibility of spending more time with her.

She laughed, and the sound was warmer and sweeter than ambrosia even as her breath frosted in the air. "Are you seriously inviting Gram on a date?"

"If it means you'll eat dinner with me tonight, I am most serious." He tried not to look like he was holding his breath.

What power this mortal woman held over him.

"All right." She shivered, making him want to offer his coat, then she opened the door to her home. "It's cold out. Come in for a minute while I ask Gram."

He stepped over the threshold, and she hurried off, the light, delicate scent of her imprinting into his mind.

Her home was far smaller than anything he was used to, but rather than making him feel confined, the warm colors and the furniture grouped for conversation and not TV gave a sense of coziness. Photos adorned the walls, some of Valentine, some of a much older woman, but most were of a couple caught in various poses against a coastline with which he was intimately familiar. He was sure he'd seen the faces of the couple before. Family members of Valentine's, most likely, but if he'd known her family, he surely would have noted Valentine herself. As he was trying to recall who they were, she reentered the room, the old woman from the photos in tow. She'd been gone the better part of half an hour and had exchanged her T-shirt for a blouse and dried her hair, which lay in a gleaming sheet of palest gold over her shoulder.

"Gram, Vittorio." She swept her arm in introduction. "Vittorio, meet my grandmother, Maria."

While they exchanged pleasantries, the identity of the couple was ticking away in the back of his mind. "These are beautiful photos." He gestured to one of them, a shot of the couple on a sailboat, and he remembered where he'd seen it. "This one is in the store too. They must be very special to you."

A shadow flickered across Valentine's eyes. "They are." Her chest rose with her sharp intake of breath. "They were my parents."

He acknowledged the past tense with a nod. Since he'd met Valentine only this morning, he had gained an alarming propensity to create awkwardness. He suddenly didn't know whether he should let his hands hang at his sides or shove them in his pockets like a hooligan, let alone attempt to produce a single sentence that wouldn't offend her. "I didn't mean to stir up painful memories."

Valentine allowed him a forgiving smile. When she reached for her coat, he mustered the presence of mind to hold it for her as she put it on. When he did the same thing for her grandmother, Valentine's smile broadened.

He bowed slightly to offer his arm to Maria. As he did, his gaze caught a flash of gold in Valentine's handbag. He recognized it immediately, as anyone descended from the gods would.

Valentine Arciere possessed Cupid's bow.

That changed everything.

"Did they hire a new chef?" Gram raised her wine glass, and Vittorio beamed and clinked his glass against Gram's as though there had indeed been a new chef hired, and it had been his idea to do so.

Val clinked hers too, hoping for Gram's sake it hadn't been a mistake not to protest when Vittorio told the waiter to bring a bottle of Quintarelli. Val had heard of the label, though she couldn't see herself ever spending that kind of money on something you drank over the course of a dinner; she hadn't expected it would go to her head this fast. Gram drank even more seldom than Val did, and she could imagine how it must be hitting her. The background noise faded to a pleasant murmur, and the lighting seemed mellower, the fabric of the table linens richer, the stemware to gleam like crystal. And through it all, the molten-insides sensation that had been plaguing her all day. Gram seemed to be enjoying the wine, so Val decided not to protest. If Vittorio wanted to blow his money, that was up to him.

In her present haze, with the candlelight gilding Vittorio's skin, she could almost believe Gram's imaginary world of gods and magical powers existed.

Yet the whisper of reality reminded her that if Gram continued to act as though she believed the golden bow in Val's purse actually had belonged to Cupid, she'd have to make her a doctor's appointment.

And then what? A series of diagnoses, prognoses, treatments... Just for that reason, part of her wished Gram could be right.

Vittorio was staring at her, and she realized he'd said something that required a response. She swallowed her mouthful of pasta, tomatoes, and herbs prepared with pure, organic Italian sunshine and forced herself to return to the real world. "Mmm?"

"Have you been to Rome?" he asked, including Gram in the question.

Val shook her head and had another careful sip of the wine. She didn't want to think about Rome, because that meant acknowledging she and Vittorio had vastly disparate lives. He would eventually return to his life in Italy while she stayed in Cupid's Hollow with only the memory of how he'd felt in her arms.

Was she actually considering getting seriously involved with a man she'd met less than twenty-four hours ago? She didn't understand what was making her think in a way that was so out of character for her.

Gram set down her fork and leaned forward, the years seeming to lift from her face. "Not for many, many years, *bello*, but now that Valentine has taken over the family business, I plan to go back soon."

"Gram?" Val hadn't taken over the business—she and Gram were equal partners—and to her knowledge Gram had never been out of the country. Nor had Gram ever spontaneously broken into Italian, especially not to call a man *bello*.

"You must visit me next time you're there." Vittorio toasted Gram again, but his dark gaze lingered on Val.

Agreeing to have dinner with him had been a mistake. Perhaps there would be a time in her life when she could enjoy romance, or even a fling, or whatever a relationship with Vittorio might look like. But that time wasn't now. Now, Gram needed her. Val had to stop thinking of her pathetic love life and get back to being the grown-up.

Her glass was almost empty. As soon as she had the thought, Vittorio filled it for what might be more than the second or third time. The wait staff, their faces new to her, had unobtrusively removed at least one empty bottle. In fact, she didn't recognize a single server tonight. It was as though, to make her decision more difficult than it already was, she had been transported from cozy Cupid's Hollow to the understated elegance of a Tuscan ristorante.

The wine must be getting to her. She took one more sip—okay, two, but it was better than anything she'd ever tasted—and set her glass aside.

"Thank you for the dinner." She pretended to glance at her watch, not caring which numbers the hands pointed at. "We should get going."

"Fiddle-faddle." Gram lunged over the table and clasped Vittorio's hand. "My Valentine is much too modest to tell you her news, but such a lovely dinner deserves to be a celebration."

One side of his mouth curved upward, but his eyes remained serious. "Indeed. And what are we celebrating?"

"Only the most important milestone in my granddaughter's life." Gram dipped her free hand into Val's purse.

Val's pulse tripped. Not the Cupid thing again, please. She grabbed for her purse but Gram was too fast. The cool metal of the miniature crossbow slid through her fingers, and Gram held up the golden instrument. It glittered in the candlelight, reflected perfectly in the darkness of Vittorio's eyes.

Paralysis gripped her as she watched Vittorio take the bow and examine it. It was *hers*, and inexplicably, it suddenly was imperative that Vittorio did not have it. But that made no sense at all. Through the pounding rush of blood in her head, she grasped for a way through these illogical feelings. When movement returned to her, she forced herself to clench her hands in her lap, telling herself the bow was merely a curiosity—valuable perhaps, but it shouldn't have such a pull on her emotions.

He caressed it. Her nails dug into her palms.

Gram scooted from her seat. "I'll be right back. You two kids enjoy yourselves."

When Gram headed for the washroom, Val reminded herself that even if Gram were experiencing some kind of dementia, these things came about gradually. Gram would be able to find her way back to the table in this small restaurant. She relaxed slightly.

Vittorio turned the bow over in his hands, his fingers long and sensuous as they stroked the curved lines. He sighted along the instrument at a wineglass and then handed it back to her. "You don't believe her."

"Pardon me?"

"It's more common than you'd think, ancestry that goes back to the gods."

"Gram can't hear you. You don't have to humor her."

"So prove me wrong."

"There's nothing to prove." Why was he playing into Gram's medical problem? "What you're suggesting is fantasy. Insanity."

"Cupid did exist, and the power of his bow is real. Whether you're a true descendant of his, though, remains to be seen."

"I am not. Descended. From the god of erotic love."

"If you're not, you'll be unable to work the bow."

"Oh, please. Even Gram can work this bow." When she thought about it, the logic of her argument didn't exactly hold water. She became aware again of the place on her shoulder where the arrow had hit her. The numbness had turned to tingling; alarmingly, it had spread to her arm.

"Case in point. Go on. Pick a target, if only to prove me wrong."

"If that's what it'll take." She eyed various patrons and let her gaze skip over a few of the wait staff. Gram still hadn't returned from the washroom, or Val would have chosen her just on principle. Keeping her hands hidden below the table, she extracted a tiny arrow-shaped bolt from the change compartment of her purse and fitted it into the bow. She adjusted the tension on the string for the close-range shot their confined surroundings required.

Still holding the bow under the table, she took aim at her target and loosed the arrow.

A look of shock spread over Vittorio's face.

She gave him her sincerest smile. "Did you really think I'd fire a weapon at an innocent bystander?"

The sights and sounds of the restaurant receded into blackness, and a rushing noise filled her head.

The little goddess had beguiled him, not even realizing what she was doing. And Vittorio, who should know better, had let her begin her transformation in a public place in full view of the mortal world.

Already he could feel the arrow's magic on him, his deity magnifying the effect to the limit of his control. His blood coursed through him hot and fast.

He was beside her, holding her close to him, yet couldn't recall leaving his seat. All he knew was that he must have her for himself, soon. And for all time.

Regardless of who or what she was, regardless of the tricks she had played to win his heart, win it she had.

"*Ti amo,*" he murmured.

For once she was supple, not protesting, and an oddly protective instinct made his chest ache. Yet he found himself cupping her chin in his hand and tilted her face toward him, intending to sample her lips before they left the restaurant.

Her head lolled. Her eyes were closed, and he could see her pulse flutter against the pale skin of her throat.

Gods. His desire for her still raged, but his disregard for her lack of consciousness hit him like a slap to the face. He didn't understand how she made him feel this way, didn't understand his feelings for her, period.

The moment of indecision gave him a chance to regroup. That she'd wielded Cupid's bow could mean only that she carried the old god's blood in her veins. That she'd blacked out after loosing the arrow meant she'd not come into her god powers yet. Of course she hadn't—apparently not learning of her heritage until today. Typical woman, to do things in whatever manner she pleased, with complete disregard for the natural order of things.

There was only one course of action available to him now to ensure Valentine survived the night. He summoned every iota of control he possessed and stopped himself from ravishing her right here and right now. Their lovemaking must wait. He must bring her to the only safe place he knew so he could help her through the transition to her god form.

four

$\mathcal{W}$ ARM, STRONG ARMS surrounded her. Her head lay on a broad chest, and the slow, steady rhythm of heartbeat thumped against her cheek. She opened her eyes. Vittorio had left his seat and was on her side of the table, supporting her in his arms.

"I got a little woozy this morning when we met too." His expression was stern, as though she'd committed some horrible faux pas. "You get used to it after a while."

She willed herself to sit up straight. That failed abysmally, and he kept an arm around her as though he had every right to do so. This close to him, every squishy, squashy thought she'd had about him flooded back through her. His thigh was heavily muscled under her hand. His pulse against her cheek hit a faster tempo. She realized it was because her hand, as though it had a mind of its own, was exploring the length of his thigh.

"You slipped something into my wine." She frantically pawed through her purse for her cell phone. "I'm calling the police."

"No to the first, *amore mio.*" His voice was like warm honey melting over her. "And no to the second."

She couldn't figure out whether that made sense, and it became more urgent to fight against the blackness that was once again encroaching on her vision.

Across the dining room, Gram finally reappeared around

the corner. Val tried again to sit upright, to escape the seductive hold in which Vittorio had trapped her. Gram paused, winked, gave Val a double thumbs-up, and disappeared back into the ladies' room, leaving her alone with Vittorio.

"Why are you doing this to me?" she whispered. He smelled so good, and though her mind protested, her body and soul longed to let him have his way with her. The attraction she'd felt to him this morning was nothing compared to this. She wanted him with an intensity that made it difficult to breathe.

He snapped his fingers, and a waiter appeared. A few words of Italian caused the waiter to produce a cell phone and place it in his hand. She heard muted electronic tones. "It's me. I have a situation." He gave a brief description of Gram and instructions to pick her up from the restaurant and deliver her home.

That seemed quite considerate... for a criminal.

She scrambled away from the table, and the floor came rushing up at her. The tile mosaic really was exquisite—and suddenly Vittorio was carrying her in his arms as he exited the restaurant. A sleek, dark car prowled to the curb, its make unfamiliar to her. The engine emitted a rumble like the sound of distant thunder, and the hairs on her arms stood up. When the driver got out and opened the back door for them, she remembered her concern about what might have been in the wine and found the presence of mind to struggle. "I need to go home. I need to call a cab."

"Don't worry," Vittorio said. "We're going somewhere private, where I can help you understand what is happening to you."

"I'm not leaving Gram!" She kicked him.

He faltered and let out a pained cough. Her kick must've gotten him where it counted. Good.

Then he deposited her in the backseat of the car and

climbed in after her, his arm shielding his groin against another well-placed—or lucky—kick.

"You have my word that both you and your grandmother will be safe." The sincerity in his voice, in his eyes, almost made her believe him.

Opaque black glass secluded them from the driver. Though the movement of the car was smooth, she had the odd feeling they were traveling much faster than a car should be able to drive through the twisting mountain roads leading from Cupid's Hollow.

She wondered if there were any connection between the name of the town and the bizarre events of the day. But that was ridiculous, because gods and goddesses didn't exist. They were myths. Hence the term *mythology*.

Vittorio sat across from her, visibly tense, and watched her as though preparing for her to spring up and attack him. It was unnerving. He'd slipped something into her wine. It had to be that. Because she just wasn't the kind of girl whose head was filled with fantasies that sucked the breath from her.

At least, not until tonight.

Just as when she'd learned days after the fact that she'd lost her parents to the sea, all sense of control had been stolen from her tonight. She didn't want to feel this desire for him that defied all logic, but no amount of arguing with herself could stop her from feeling it.

That didn't mean she was about to give up, though. She reminded herself that hooking up with Vittorio might feel good while it lasted, but these things always ended in heartache.

She had somehow crept forward in her seat and swayed closer to him. She jammed herself back against the door panel. "Where did you say we're going?"

He consulted his watch. "Let's not spoil the surprise. You'll see in a few moments."

She felt more alert now, less mentally fuzzy. Thankfully, whatever had been in the wine must be wearing off. But that made her current situation even less tolerable. The leather seat was sensuous against her skin. The air carried a musky, tantalizing scent so intense she could taste it. Despite the subdued lighting, every detail of Vittorio's face became vividly clear, from the aristocratic planes of his cheekbones and nose to the strong arches of his eyebrows to the masculine firmness of his mouth. Her breathing quickened. As she caught herself sliding toward him again, his pupils dilated and his skin flushed. An answering rush of warmth flooded her chest.

The sensation of motion ceased, and Vittorio's gaze flicked to the door. It silently swung open.

Sunlight glared into the car, disorienting her. She blinked as her eyes adjusted, and Vittorio exited the vehicle. He leaned back in and offered her his hand. "We are here, amore mio."

Her heart beat faster than it should. How could two little words have such an effect on her? Hoping he couldn't feel that she was quivering inside, she accepted his hand and stepped out of the car.

They stood on a mountaintop overlooking an azure sea, and the breeze that swept over her was rich with the scents of olives and lemons. The sun blazed from the horizon. Val's pulse throbbed in her temples. She didn't recognize their exact location, but the clusters of cube-like white dwellings on the flanks of the hills, roofs tiled with the distinctive orange of terra-cotta, meant they could be nowhere other than the Mediterranean.

Which was impossible to drive to in a car.

Was this where *Salacia* had slipped under the waves? Were her parents' bodies somewhere in those blue depths?

The limo rolled away without sound over the cobbled ground.

Sudden dizziness made her bend over and clutch her knees.

Vittorio was at her side in an instant, placing a steadying hand on her back. "Easy," he said, his tone soothing as though he were calming a panicked animal. "It will pass. Take deep breaths."

She felt the blood gradually return to her head, and her vision cleared enough for her to stand. The vista hadn't changed, only gained detail as the sun edged over the gently rounded mountaintops. She found her cell phone in her purse and stared at the time and date displayed, noting the no-signal notification as she did a quick mental calculation of time zones. They'd arrived at the restaurant in Cupid's Hollow at around eight o'clock last night, February 1. Allowing an hour for dinner, she came to an inescapable conclusion: somehow they'd traveled across a minimum of six time zones in the space of fifteen minutes.

The lush scent of this place, the warmth of the breeze on her skin, the brilliance of the sun, the solidity of the cobbles under her feet, the distant *scree* of sea birds… It was too real for this to be a dream. So either the business about gods was real or she was hallucinating. Maybe the stress of seeing what might be her parents' eternal resting place had been enough to crack her mind completely.

Vittorio's hand caressed the small of her back. "Come, amore mio. I will show you our home." His voice thickened. His gaze offered a promise she couldn't resist. Despite the spiraling grief inside of her—and the very real chance that either she had lost her mind or he had dosed her like a cat— she wanted to go with him. She needed to be with him.

He turned her, his palm resting against the small of her back, intimate and somehow comforting. White stone columns stretched toward the sky, adorning a vast temple. The home of a god. Her breath left her in an appreciative sigh.

But this wasn't… couldn't be… real.

She backed up a step, caught her heel in the cobbles, bent and yanked her shoes from her feet in case she needed to run. "I'm not going to do this."

Whatever *this* was.

"You must complete your transformation." An implacable edge tinged his voice and hardened his jaw. Despite the clear sky, the air tasted of electricity. "You are the issue of the gods. You must accept this."

So when he wasn't getting his way, she wasn't his amore anymore? Val shook her head. She stumbled backward another step.

Vittorio crossed his arms over his chest. His nostrils flared. His eyes glittered dangerously. "Your transformation requires you to take a lover or to take a life."

Did he really assume she'd stay here and participate in this craziness?

But if it was crazy, then how had she crossed a continent and an ocean in the blink of an eye?

Didn't matter. It wasn't real, and she wasn't sticking around for any more of it.

She whirled around and started walking. She didn't care that she didn't have a specific destination in mind, as long as she got away from here. Grit and pebbles dug into the soles of her feet with each step as though in an attempt to convince her Vittorio had told her the truth, that she was really on a hilltop over the Mediterranean, in the company of a god.

No footsteps pursued her.

With her shoes in one hand and her purse in the other, she ran toward the track that led from this place toward the village far below. Wherever he had taken her, surely there would be sane people who could tell her where she was, and then she could call Gram and arrange to get back home.

At the edge of the cobbles she met an invisible resistance, as though the air had somehow become thick, almost solid. Her limbs floundered and slowed. Running became impossible. She dragged her legs forward, but the resistance increased until she couldn't move in any direction but back. Back toward the temple. Back toward Vittorio.

Gasping with the exertion of her failed flight, she stormed across the cobbles and stopped inches away from him. Everything about him was beautiful, from his physical appearance to the way she felt so right just being with him. This inexplicable longing for him terrified her; if there were any truth to the story of Cupid's bow, how could she trust her feelings—or his?

"What *was* that?" She pointed a shaking hand at the invisible barrier.

"The property has a"—he squeezed the bridge of his nose between his thumb and forefinger—"you might call it a force field."

"Well, turn it off."

"I cannot."

"You can't be serious."

"When you entered in a state of flux, you triggered it. It's a safeguard."

In a state of flux? Her? After what she'd just been through, *flux* was too tame a word. More like *losing her freaking mind.* "A safeguard against what?"

A muscle in his neck twitched. "You."

Her throat ached and her eyes stung with the effort of holding in her frustration.

"Please." Despite her best efforts to remain calm, her voice wavered. "I don't want to be here."

Hurt flickered in his eyes. "You have made that clear.

And now let me make something clear to you. You cannot return to the mortal world in your present state."

"And what state might that be? Kidnapped?" She didn't entirely believe that, but of all the possible options, the one that seemed blatantly obvious was too bizarre to believe. Gods didn't exist.

He groaned. "Do you not see what's right in front of you?"

All too well. And if gods didn't exist, nothing that had happened to Val since this morning made any sense whatsoever. She didn't want to believe, but… "I'm trying to."

"Until you complete your transformation from mortal to goddess, your form is too unstable for you to remain in the mortal world."

"Let me get this straight. You're saying that I need to either make love with you or kill you—since you seem to be the only candidate around—because if I don't, I'd what, disintegrate?"

"You've heard of the destruction of the library of Alexandria, no? The flood in Noah's time?"

She pressed the heels of her hands to her temples. Fine. She'd play along. "So what do I do?"

"I assume you know Cupid's area of expertise."

How could she not know? Even if she hadn't—and assuming, which she didn't, that his preposterous tale was in any way connected to reality—she'd have figured it out from the way her body reacted to Vittorio's. "Cupid was supposedly the god of erotic love."

"Not supposedly."

"Great. You're saying the only thing that will get me out of here is to round up a bunch of virile young men and have an orgy? Your logic fails you there, because you're the only guy I see hanging around."

Vittorio harrumphed. He clamped his hands around her upper arms and gave her a firm shake. "That is most certainly *not* what I'm saying. Do you think the king of gods would share his woman?"

"Whoa, buddy." She jabbed a finger against his chest. He was harder, more powerful than a man should be. *Because he's a god?* Yet even with him manhandling her, even though she was trapped here by a means that couldn't possibly be real, she couldn't feel anything but safe. And incredibly attracted to him. Or was that the effect of the arrow—or the wine? "I am not *your* anything."

"You are. You just don't accept it yet." A blood vessel pulsed at his temple, and the obvious effort it cost him to restrain himself was more than a little alarming.

"I don't intend to find out, either." She pulled away. He didn't try to stop her.

"Why do you resist your destiny?"

"Destiny is for people who can't think for themselves."

He shook his head. "Destiny is for people who are meant to be together."

There he went again, saying things that made her want to leap into his embrace and forget everything but the way he made her heart flutter.

"I'm sorry. I know you believe what you're saying." She touched her fingertips to the ache in her chest. "But even if it's true, it's wrong to manipulate someone's feelings. I don't want to go through my life wondering whether what I feel for you—or you for me—is real or just some side effect of that stupid bow."

She turned away and looked down over the sea. Anywhere but at Vittorio, whose mere presence turned her into someone she didn't even know. She forced herself not to think of him, just for a moment. Somewhere in the blue depths lay her parents. Had their love been real? Or was it a manipulation of Cupid's bow? She would never know because they were gone.

When she realized she was actually considering that Cupid's bow could be a reality, she felt woozy again.

She didn't want to be here, didn't want to deal with the loss of her parents all over again, didn't want to deal with the idea of gods and goddesses that Vittorio and Gram seemed bent on convincing her were true. She turned and glared at him. "Just leave me alone."

No wonder his best people had been unable to convince her to sell her store. He had never met anyone, man or woman, mortal or god, so stubborn. Yet underlying her obstinacy was a vulnerability that made him want to protect her from harm, and from the sadness that lingered in her eyes and her voice when she spoke of love. Even the lines of her body spoke eloquently of the strength of her beliefs.

But he was of Jupiter's line, and his will would prevail in all things. Right now, even more important than furthering his empire or slaking his desire for her, he needed to show Valentine Arciere the sincerity of his feelings for her.

Egad. He had feelings for her. Feelings that went far beyond physical attraction, though she was the most attractive woman he'd ever met. Feelings that made him want to protect her, made him want to make her happy, made him want to put her needs before his own. *Feelings.*

Well, so be it.

He would woo her.

The thought sent his pulse pounding, and his blood pressure shot up painfully in the most sensitive area of his body.

The sun was beginning to warm the cobbles, and heat rose up around them. Sweat prickled his scalp. Valentine, not yet in her goddess form, must be uncomfortable. "Would you like to come in from the heat?" he asked solicitously, offering his arm.

She gave him a baleful glare, at odds with the delicate

flush of her skin that made her attraction to him obvious. "I suppose I don't have a choice."

"You do." When she did not take his arm, he lowered it. "Will you join me?" Then he added, "Please."

"No, thanks. I prefer the sun." She turned half away from him once more to gaze over the sea, and the sun's brilliant light silhouetted her well-formed figure through the thin fabric of her blouse.

Vittorio drew a long breath through his nose and let it out slowly through his mouth. By rights, she belonged to him. He could do what his body demanded, take her here and now. He could see now that from the moment he met her, even when he believed she was a mere mortal, he'd known she was the only woman who could ever make him complete. Until then, he'd thought nothing lacked from his life. He had all the pleasures wealth could bring, and Jupitropolis dominated the world financially and culturally. He did what he pleased. Until now. Because now he understood that the one thing that would truly please him... he couldn't simply *do*.

Nor, she had proved, could her affection be bought.

Sweat dampened her clothing and made her blouse cling to her, which made keeping his hands off her more difficult than ever. The sun's rays had begun to pinken her February-pale skin, yet she'd refused his offer of shelter. She didn't seem to value creature comforts.

Thus far, the only things she appeared to care about were her grandmother, though he'd assured her Maria's safety was not at issue, and knowing whether she could trust the attraction between Vittorio and herself.

If he was going to woo her—and he was—he would have to woo her with what she valued most.

Trust.

He would place his life in her hands.

five

A NAGGING DISCOMFORT HAD been swelling inside Val. It wasn't due to the heat or the beginnings of what surely would turn into a painful sunburn. It wasn't even due to the fact that she'd been kidnapped—though, if she were going to be honest with herself, she didn't believe anymore that Vittorio had forced her to come here against her will. Or if he had, her lapse of judgment in shooting a god with Cupid's bow had a lot to do with everything that had happened since the moment she'd squeezed the trigger.

Feeling temperamental, she bit her lip just to hear the hitch she'd discovered that small action caused in Vittorio's breathing. He hadn't pressed her further since she'd turned down his offer to go with him into his temple. The cool darkness she would find within it certainly was tempting, but that was nowhere close to the mounting temptation to give in to this raw need she felt for him. Crossing that threshold would mean giving in, and that scared her. At least staying out in the sun gave her some small sense of control. She tried not to imagine what it would feel like to belong there with him. Their home, he'd called it, as though she'd already said yes to a proposal he'd never uttered. She wasn't falling for that. But… she knew in her heart that he wasn't lying about the whole goddess thing. And that scared her almost as much as her attraction to him did. "How bad will it get if we don't…?"

"One of us will die," he said, way too calmly.

She clenched and unclenched her hands and wrapped her arms around herself. She paced. She stood still. She tried deep breathing. But she felt as though something within her was shifting, or was about to shift, like a seismic rumbling that preceded a landslide.

"Why?"

He looked at her as though she were two years old and failed to understand the most rudimentary of concepts. "Because I will not allow you to kill us both."

She wouldn't kill *anybody*. Couldn't. If anything were true, it was that. "Are you saying you'll stand by and watch… whatever this is… destroy me?"

The distance between them increased as he took a step backward. His arms rose slightly from his sides, and his stance grew alert and ready. "Because you have inherited Cupid's power, your transformation comes with a unique condition. If you choose not to take a lover, the transformation will be too powerful for you to control." Until she noticed him tracking her movements with his eyes, she hadn't realized she was weaving side to side, seeking some impalpable advantage over him. He held up a palm to her. "One of us will die. I prefer for it not to be you."

If she chose not to take a lover, she would die. And he was the only one available here inside his force field. Oh, now that was convenient for him. "However I might feel about you, I'm not going to kill you. Or anyone."

"When the change comes upon you, you will not be able to control it, and it will drain itself in violence."

"Unless we become lovers," she reminded him.

He nodded. "Some people would see that as the wiser choice."

"Don't you dare try to put this on me. I didn't ask for any of this Cupid stuff. I don't even believe in it. This morning I was minding my own business in my store, and now… Don't you see? Love is supposed to be about respect and trust, not magic and controlling people. I don't even know you, and because of that stupid arrow, all I want is to—to—" A sob convulsed in her throat. "It's like some awful nightmare I can't wake up from."

Once more, hurt flashed in his eyes. She hadn't meant that the idea of loving him was nightmarish to her—just the opposite—but she could tell that's how he'd taken it. It was the loss of control over her emotions that she couldn't bear. Everything she'd believed in, everything she'd trusted, had vanished.

Without planning to, she lunged toward him. Caught herself before clawing his face.

His mouth twitched. His expression remained grim. "The situation is less than ideal for me too."

"You're really willing to risk your life. For me. You don't even know me." He was unbelievable.

"The transformation requires that you divert its energy into another person one way or another." He held out his hands to her. "I place my life in your hands, Valentine, to show you the trust you so desperately seek."

She wanted to believe what he said. Wanted to trust him. But after all she'd seen today, trust was the least logical place she could go right now.

Her uncertainty swirled in a maelstrom of logic and desire. Her need for release burgeoned until she had to clamp her jaws together to keep from screaming. It would be easy to give in to him now, to let his touch soothe away the unbearable pressure inside her.

But her mind could not accept what her heart insisted was true. What if she had an advantage because of her resistance to believe what was happening? Maybe she could control it if she tried hard enough.

"I'm sorry," she whispered.

"I know." Sorrow settled over his face, the set of his shoulders, like a heavy mantle. "I shall bear the force of the transformation that you may survive it."

For a fleeting moment, she clung to the hope that none of this was real. Then the awful power within her awakened. It surged through her, seeking prey on which to sate itself.

She bent and drove her fingers into the cobbled ground and wrenched a stone from its bed. The solid weight of the rock in her hand belied the surreality of what she had just done. She hefted it, feeling its deadly potential. Now that it was too late, she believed what Vittorio had said about how the transformation would control her. Tears blurred her vision. She blinked them away as she fitted the stone, which had transformed into a deadly bolt, into the golden bow without allowing herself to think about how it should not be possible. Instinct aimed it at Vittorio's heart.

He ducked as she loosed the stone bolt, and it hurtled through the air where he had stood a moment before. It struck one of the pillars at the front of the temple, blasting away a chunk the size of a car.

She screamed a wordless battle cry and clawed another stone from the ground, shattering its neighbors, horrified by what she was doing but unable to stop herself.

Vittorio bowed slightly, never letting his gaze stray from her, and resumed his defensive stance. "It begins, amore mio."

The second stone bolt hit his shoulder and knocked him backward, a flash of blue light exploding from his flesh. His face paled. Her senses sharpened. Every moment brought greater strength and speed and heightened the bloodlust coiled in her belly. She plucked up stones to use in her bow as easily as though they were pebbles, and loosed shot after shot.

Vittorio was fast, and behind him the massive stone temple bore her punishment until the columns and walls and roof crumbled, thundering to the ground amid choking clouds of dust.

If she had only her mortal senses, she suspected she would be unable to perceive his movements. But her accuracy was better than it had ever been, and her next shot struck his chest. Another blinding blue flash crackled through the air.

The stone shattered, pieces clattering to the ground, and Vittorio fell to his knees.

She raised another stone and readied the bow.

His gaze held hers, deep and sincere and steady, though the deadliest of weapons was aimed at his heart. She couldn't look away from him. This man, whom she hardly knew, who hardly knew her, was willing to die for her. The enormity of that sacrifice made her hands shake.

The bow wavered.

"Is it done?" she begged. *Please, please, let it be done.* But she paced toward him. The tip of the bow rested against his chest, rising and falling with each ragged breath he took.

"The power is at its peak. It must be drained." His shirt had torn, and where the bow touched him, a dark bruise stained his skin. She had done that to him. She had hurt him because she'd refused to trust him though he offered his life as proof that she could. The life of not just a man but a god, in exchange for a simple act of trust.

He wasn't the monster. She was.

"I'm sorry," she said again. Her finger began to squeeze the trigger. She couldn't make it stop. All she could do was back up one step. But it would not be enough to save him. "I don't want to do this."

"I know, Valentine." He swayed on his knees but never looked away from her. "I understand."

The mechanism of the bow engaged. Time seemed to expand as the arrow sprang from its seat. Millimeter by millimeter the string thrust it on its killing trajectory. The full power of her transformation was finally released, and she screamed as it rushed from her in blinding shards of light.

In that instant, she gained control of her body.

The bolt left the bow.

She dove forward, pushing her hand toward the blaze of gold in what she knew was a hopeless attempt to knock it aside.

Agony sliced through her forearm, and she thudded to the ground.

Silence and darkness descended around her.

six

VALENTINE FLOATED ON the darkness. Gradually the outside world crept in; her arm felt like it was on fire, and Vittorio was muttering nearby. She couldn't be sure what he said because he was speaking Italian, but it sounded like a string of invectives. She opened her eyes.

The sun had descended over the horizon and streaked the sky with lush crimson and violet. The glaring heat had faded, and the air was soft, fragrant with citrus.

Vittorio gently smoothed green salve over a gash her forearm, numbing the pain. If not for the wound, she might almost believe she hadn't attacked him, hadn't been overcome by a crazed urge to annihilate the one person who was trying to help her.

She pushed herself up to a sitting position. Vittorio reached over to where Cupid's bow lay on the ground a few feet away and slid it out of her reach. "How do you feel?"

Rolling her shoulders, she evaluated her physical condition. Other than the cut on her arm, which, on further inspection, seemed no more than a scratch, she didn't seem to have suffered any ill effects from the morning's bizarre activities. "Okay, I think."

"For a time I feared I had lost you."

"From this?" She held up her arm. The scratch faded to nothing. As she watched it, the backs of her arms prickled and her chest felt uncomfortably warm. She turned her wrist, and the muscles moved freely under the smooth new skin. "How…?"

He shrugged. "It's basic first aid. Godhood 101."

The god world collided again with her normal, sane life and left her trembling. "There's actual god school?"

"No." He chuckled as he set aside the salve, which he'd been dabbing from a cupped piece of stone that might once have been part of a fluted column. Another smooth stone lay nearby, one of its sides stained green, as well as several bunches of herbs. He had defended himself from her, taking her attacks and never retaliating, and then nursed her with medicine he'd made with his own hands. "But you tend to pick up a few skills along the way."

A puff of a breeze fluttered the shreds of his torn shirt, revealing the painful-looking bruises she had inflicted on him. He looked like he'd survived a bombing. Barely. Deep inside her, the horrible stirring reawakened. "Will that… what happened before… can it happen again?"

She found herself calculating the distance to the bow.

He leveled a wary gaze at her and subtly shifted his posture to put himself between her and the weapon. "I think you know the answer to that."

"I believe you." She sucked in a deep breath. Gram, who clearly was not suffering from dementia, had tried to tell her. Vittorio had tried to tell her. Yet it had taken nearly killing him for her to accept that what they'd told her was the truth. She should try not to be so resistant to learning about her new role, no matter how difficult that may prove. Her pulse rushed in her ears so she could hardly hear herself speaking. "And… I trust you."

He caught her hands and let them rest on his palms. "You always could."

"I know that now." She dabbed her finger into the salve and traced it across his chest. At first he flinched, and then as the herbs did their work and the discoloration faded, along with the last of the day's light, he sighed deeply. She leaned closer to him. Placed her palm against his face. A new kind of seismic shift happened between them. She bit her lower lip, and his breath caught.

"Are you sure you want this?" His voice grew thick and husky, this man who had been willing to give up everything for her sake. That was what had made her deflect the arrow at the last moment. His actions had been borne of selflessness, in order to show her she could trust him. And she did, with all her heart.

"I've never been surer of anything." She moved onto his lap and continued exploring his chest and arms with her hands as he crushed her to him. With difficulty, she pushed back from him so she could look into his eyes. "And you're positive this will not harm you?"

He laughed, a low, happy sound that sent a tingle from her belly to the tips of her toes. "I'm most certain this will not harm either of us."

With decadent caresses over her mouth, her face, her throat, her arms, he gently lowered her to her back. Under the wheeling constellations, he loved her, the dark locks of his hair trailing across her shoulders, and she buried her fingers in the thick mass of it so she could pull his lips closer to hers.

Without warning, the power of the transformation surged through her again. She cried out and tensed. What if he were wrong? What if she lost control again?

Vittorio murmured unintelligible words of reassurance and did marvelous things to her with his mouth and his hands until she relaxed again. This time the god power swelled around her and through her like music. This time it felt pure and good and right. She moaned softly.

"Amore mio," he whispered.

She could see the thread that bound them together, a glittering cord of emotion between her soul and his.

"Oh, god," she said afterward.

"Oh, god, indeed."

As the aftershocks of their lovemaking dissipated, the earth echoed with a tremor like a satisfied sigh.

Hours later, after they had made love twice more and the rubble of the temple had rumbled and settled until they had all but disappeared, the sun rose and kissed their skin with its warming rays.

The car returned as silently as it had left the night before, from where she wasn't sure, and Val scrambled to find her clothing. Vittorio laughed as he caught her and scooped her up in his arms, dropping kiss after kiss on her bare shoulder. She squirmed free.

"The driver." She spotted a scrap of cloth and snatched it up with her back to the car, trying to pull the remnants of her blouse over her arms.

"An illusion," he said. The doors of the car all opened simultaneously, confirming that there was no driver inside. Across the backseat lay fresh clothes for both of them. Vittorio leaned in to get them, then grinned as he laid across her arms a blouse made of the silkiest fabric she had ever touched, and a pair of leather pants as soft and smooth as butter. "But the perks are real."

She pulled the garments over her limbs, luxuriating in the feel of them. The leather would be too warm for the heat of this climate, but she assumed they'd be getting back into the magical car soon enough. When she finished dressing, she ran her fingers through her hair to get out the worst of the tangles. Vittorio had gotten into his clothes faster than she did hers, in that annoying way men do, and now leaned against the side of the car, blatantly admiring her. She smiled to herself behind her hair. She could get used to this.

He'd tied his hair at his nape, revealing the well-formed features of, well, a god. Just looking at him made her want to fling off her clothes and spend the day making love with him. She stepped toward him.

He drew a sharp breath as he enfolded her in his arms and stroked her hair. "We must go back, amore mio. Even a god needs to rest after a night like that one."

A few last stones shifted and rolled off the remains of the temple, emitting a dusty sigh as though reprimanding her for the ferocity of last night. He was right. As relieved as Val was to have survived the transformation from mortal to goddess, as wonderful as the aftermath of that had been, she had her life back in Cupid's Hollow to get back to. Gram. Her business.

"I'll get the bow, then we can go." She bit her lip. "Is it safe for me to touch it now?"

He brought her hands to his mouth and kissed each fingertip, sending shivers of anticipation through her. "I trust you will remain in control of the bow's power."

Struck deeply by his choice of words, she picked it up, along with her purse, which lay nearby. The workmanship of the bow was just as amazing as she'd found it the day before. When she'd first handled it, before shooting Vittorio, it had had no effect on her, and she'd hoped that might be how it worked now. But she was wrong. It seemed almost alive with contained power, as though it desired to be used in the machinations of the gods as they influenced mortal lives. She wasn't sure she liked that, and she tucked it far into her purse, which now had the soft gleam of gold. Evidently it had transformed itself into an accessory befitting a goddess.

As she walked back to Vittorio, the sunlight glittered off the slender golden thread stretched from her heart to his. She blinked, but it didn't go away. She decided not to ask Vittorio about it just yet; despite the wondrousness of entering the world of the gods, the morning's light brought the age-old morning-after questions for her to mull over during the brief trip home, and she needed time to think.

He'd said he was thinking of moving to Cupid's Hollow. But now everything had changed. Would he tire of small-town life and expect her to leave with him? Or had she let herself be dazzled by thoughts of immortality and fallen into a one-night stand? And what about the conversation they'd had yesterday in her shop? He was firmly on the side of big business. Well, that was one thing she wouldn't budge on.

As the car pulled up in front of the sports shop, a cell phone rang from the console. Vittorio checked it, frowned, and sent a brief text message. He dropped it back into his pocket, a second thread of light flaring and then fading till she could see only the one connecting him to her. She couldn't put her finger on how she knew it, but suddenly a faint discord emanated from him.

The sun was just brightening the pale sky here in Cupid's Hollow, and the empty storefronts looked dark and bleak. Deb's son was hunched in his parka, bow case leaning beside her door, waiting for her to open up early for his archery lesson.

Feeling more and more uncertain of how her relationship with Vittorio was supposed to work here in the real world, Val kissed him on the cheek. "Back to the daily grind?"

He slid on a pair of sunglasses, and though he smiled at her, the dark glasses concealed his eyes so she couldn't discern his true emotion. A ray of sunlight pierced the darkness of the car's interior, its brightness masking the glittering thread between them. "We both must attend to our tasks here. But I would very much like to take you out to dinner again."

"I'd like that too." Her relief surprised her, and she realized that she would have been devastated if he'd simply left and never called again. She waved as the car left with him, and then she greeted her pupil and unlocked the shop, the bell above the door tinkling.

Something Vittorio said earlier tickled her mind. He was the descent of the god Jupiter. For him not to be involved with Jupitropolis defied credulity. Her heart told her she could trust him without doubt... but she was the only thing standing between him and (if her instinct could be trusted) his new megastore. How far would a man as powerful as Vittorio go to get what he wanted?

Vittorio leaned back in the seat of the car and tried to get his thoughts in order. A pair of women strutted past on the sidewalk, and although he noticed them, he hadn't the slightest inclination to bed either one of them. In fact, just the thought of any woman sent his mind straight to Valentine. Something must be the matter with him. Perhaps it would pass.

What if it didn't?

He caught himself smiling like a fool. Well, perhaps it wouldn't pass. He could think of worse things. Like the Jupitropolis board meeting, which would be videoconferenced via the device that had appeared in the car's console. He hit Randy's number on the contact list and put the phone to his ear.

"Tori, think about investing in an ear hair clipper, man."

He pulled the phone from the side of his head and pointed the camera aperture at the floor while he stuck a finger in his ear to check for ear hair, and found none. "Jerk."

His assistant grinned at him from the screen. Different color shirt today, same ridiculous Hawaiian print. Vittorio allowed himself a sigh. Sometimes he missed the simpler days when messages were sent by courier. Or pigeon.

"Have you heard from the audit people yet?"

"Relax, man. Everything's going to be fine."

"Good. I haven't seen Bacchus around, and that usually means he's up to no good. Keep an eye on Valentine for me this morning. Make sure nothing happens to her."

Randy saluted. "You're the boss."

Yes, he was. And as such, it had been his call to ensure Valentine Sports was audited. That was before he met Valentine. Before he learned he'd set events in motion that could lead to her losing her soul. Calling off the audit was the least he could do. Would that it were enough.

How he wished he'd never made that bet with Bacchus.

"Boss?"

Vittorio pulled his attention back to the business at hand. Randy was saying something about the board meeting being rescheduled because of weather. He eyed the blustery day through the dark glass of the car. It was getting bad out there, even for February in Canada. He'd become so enamored of Valentine that he'd been remiss in his duties. Something was definitely the matter with him. This time, the thought made him smile.

seven

"Hey, Scott." Val unlocked the shop door. "Been practicing?"

He broke out into a grin that covered his entire freckled face. "Yep. Wait'll you see."

She had never understood what made the boy's father walk away from his wife and son. Scott was a great kid, and Deb was smart and kind and funny—not to mention beautiful. Of course, Val had a best friend's bias about Deb, but still. Life was fragile, and love rare—look at how Val's parents had enjoyed such a fleeting time of joy together. How could someone just throw that away? Poor Deb. Poor Scott.

She ushered him in out of the cold and locked the door again. Mornings were for lessons, and the shop wouldn't open for two more hours. She reached for the light switch, but a glimmer around Scott made her stop and stare. A multitude of light threads emanated from him. Most were thin; they faded to nothing a few feet away from him. Two were long, disappearing through two of the shop's walls. Those two gave a strong, steady glow. And one of them was connected to her.

"You want to go downstairs to the range and get set up?" She shooed him toward the stairs, keeping a wary eye on the thread between them. "I'll be down in a minute."

Scott trotted off, the thread fading somewhat, and she called home. The phone rang and rang. She tried not to worry. Vittorio had assured her his people would get Gram home safely, and she knew Gram wasn't off her rocker, was of sounder mind than most people half her age. So if she wasn't answering the phone, she was probably out at a friend's house or in the washroom or doing one of any number of things normal, sane people do. But right now Val needed to hear her grandmother's voice. When she did, the jolt of relief was as welcome as a double shot of espresso.

"I believe you," she said quickly, needing to have this conversation before Scott got bored and came back upstairs. "Can you tell me about the glowing threads?"

Gram was silent for so long, Val thought the call had dropped. Then she heard a breath being released. "You can see them? Oh. Oh boy."

"Oh boy what?" The silence tied her stomach in a knot. "Gram, what's going on? Are they good? Bad?"

"Um." Gram cleared her throat. "Not bad. You haven't told anyone about being able to see them, have you?"

"No. Why?" Gram had said they weren't bad. But she hadn't said they were good. What did that mean?

"Don't. Not ever, do you understand?" Never had Gram spoken with such finality. It made Val shiver. "Swear it to me, child."

"Sure, Gram. But—"

"How did your date with that handsome man go?"

She felt her lips curve, and she decided to let the topic of the threads drop. For now. Was there any way to tell one's grandmother about lovemaking that had literally shaken the earth? "We're going on a second date."

Gram's delighted laughter buoyed her a little. Then she said she had to go or she'd be late for her hair appointment. And that she might drop in at the travel agency.

So she was serious about that. Val tried not to feel sad as she made a mental list of things she'd need to do, like hire someone to take Gram's place after she retired. She replaced her phone in her sleek new purse and went to stow it in the office.

The light was on. She pushed open the door. Scott, who apparently had the attention span of a two-year-old, had come back upstairs and was kneeling by the stack of boxes of miniature arrows.

She made a horrified sound. In slow motion, Scott whirled, ducking his head and raising his eyes in the classic pose of someone caught where he should not be. One of Cupid's arrows rested in his left hand. As he turned toward her, his fingers curled around it.

She lunged toward him. She could make it in time... as soon as that superhuman burst of goddess power hit...

But it didn't.

Scott flinched and opened his hand. The arrow had disappeared. A tiny nick on his palm healed in the half a second it took him to look down at it.

His young face rearranged itself into an expression of puppy love, and he clambered to his feet and laid his gangling hands on her waist. "Hey, Ms. Arciere. I am *so* ready for my lesson."

The line of light connecting them gained a frenetic energy.

"Whoa there, buster. Um. I actually... got an unexpected phone call, and now I have to go to... a thing." She extricated herself from his sweaty teenage grasp. "So sorry, I need to cancel your lesson for today. Besides, this is the wrong place, wrong time... wrong generation." She hoped the reference to their age difference would gently knock some sense into him.

"Oh, yeah." He winked at her. "Sure. But after my birthday next week I'll be sixteen, so—"

"Sit, please." She pointed to her chair, and he complied. She backed up with her palm toward him as though she could prevent him from rising with just a gesture. "There's been some, uh, weird sunspot activity, and they say it's making people act strangely."

Please let him buy that.

"Sunspot activity." He raised one eyebrow and lowered the other. "Right."

"Absolutely. So. I think it might be a good idea to reschedule your lesson for a couple of days from now until all that's passed."

"But—"

"But nothing. Business as usual next week, all right?"

His face crumpled, and she felt like the kind of person who stole teddy bears from toddlers. But Cupid's arrows or not, she couldn't let her best friend's teenage son have romantic feelings for her.

She lowered her hand and backed away far enough to give him a clear path to the door.

He stood, his head lowered and his chin jutting at an angle that suggested he hadn't bought the sunspot story at all. "All right, Val."

"Ms. Arciere." She tried to say it kindly. He was a nice kid, and all of this was her fault. She should have kept a better eye on the arrows. Today she'd keep the office door locked until she found a safer place to keep them.

"All right, Val," he said again. Then he stopped in front of her. As quick as only a teenager can be, he aimed a kiss at her mouth.

She managed to duck fast enough that it landed on her cheek. "That's enough."

"I'll wait till you're ready. I promise." His voice and his eyes burned with the intensity of young love for a long moment before he swung away and loped out the front door, leaving a gust of chilly wind in his wake.

Val gave him a chance to get a good distance away. Then she locked the office, hung the Be Back Soon sign on the entrance door and locked that, and headed for Gram's favorite hair salon.

There had *better* be a way to undo this.

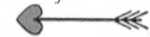

The sharp scent of perm solution mingled with the sound of scissors snipping hair and the chatter of women who made it their business to know everyone else's. Val spotted Gram, freshly cut and styled, sitting under the dryer, and she rushed to take the vacant seat beside her.

But it wasn't like she could shout her predicament over the noise of the dryer in the middle of a crowded hair salon. Adorable though the ladies might be, this place was the seat of all gossip.

Someone lifted her hair from her shoulder. "You desperately need a trim." Sonia, the salon's owner, clucked at the condition of her hair. "You're in luck, I have ten minutes before my next appointment."

Shouldn't a goddess be exempt from split ends?

Before Val could protest, Sonia herded her into a chair and draped a cloth over her, then began spritzing her with a spray bottle.

She gave up. "Just a little off the ends."

"I heard *somebody* has a new boyfriend." The salon fell silent. Comb, comb, *snip*. Her stomach dropped like an elevator. Teenage boys bragged about their conquests whether they made them or not. And if poor Scott was reacting to the arrow the same way she and Vittorio had... "All the way from Italy."

She felt a big, goofy, relieved smile spread over her face. Vittorio. Imagine if the ladies got their tongues wagging about what had really happened between them last night. And thank the gods—funny how easily that expression came to mind—this conversation was taking the direction it was taking. "Well, it was just one date."

"Girls," Sonia called out, "Maria's little Valentine roped herself a hot Italian stallion."

Val blushed ferociously and the salon twittered over her for the rest of the ten minutes it took Sonia to trim her hair. By the time Sonia dusted her off and lowered the chair, Gram's hair was dry and she'd made the rounds of the salon. Twice. Val tipped Sonia, and she and Gram left amid a fanfare of cheers.

Morning had brightened the snowy street, but the empty storefront windows of the businesses that had sold out stood black and gloomy. That was their choice, she reminded herself. They'd sold out. She linked her arm through Gram's as they walked along the deserted sidewalk. Finally they could talk.

"I had a bit of an incident with one of the arrows this morning," she confessed.

"Did you scratch yourself?" Gram flapped her hand. "Don't worry about it. Your own magic won't have an effect on you now that you've transformed."

Good to know. "It wasn't me. It was Scott."

Gram stopped in her tracks and blinked up at her, her eyes huge behind the new glasses. "Which arrow did he use?"

"How should I know? There are boxes and boxes of the things."

"Pppft!" Gram stomped. "Did he get horny or did he get angry, child?"

"He's a fifteen-year-old boy, what do you think?" Gram had said *horny*?

"It's no laughing matter. How did his demeanor change?"

"Uh... He started acting like he had a crush on me."

"Where is he now?"

"I sent him home. I suppose he's at school by now." At her grandmother's horrified expression, the hairs on the back of her neck stood erect. "Gram, what's going to happen to him? What should I do?"

"Move to another town and change your name," Gram muttered, marching toward the store at a brisk clip, her sensible shoes clopping against the sidewalk.

"What?" Val hurried after her. "Gram?"

"I told you it's no laughing matter. You need to reverse the effect of the love arrow with a hate arrow. Maybe you can catch him before he does something regrettable."

"Hate arrow. What?" It was like one of those wretched dreams in which she found herself in the middle of a class on quantum physics where everyone expected her to know what she was doing, but then suddenly she was racing through a corridor, desperately needing her textbook, and she couldn't remember where her locker was.

"Didn't you read the instructions in the box?"

"I didn't exactly have time." They'd reached the shop, where a small crowd of customers milled around the door. That was odd. Business had never been brisk this early in the day. Val stepped gingerly through them, not wanting to disturb the faintly glowing threads emanating from them, unlocked the door, and let them rush in. She had the oddest sense of *knowing*. Not that she didn't know most of her customers by name, but this was different. She could feel a deeper understanding of what each one felt at his or her core, and knew which person was grieving, who was celebrating, conniving, or smug. No one seemed intent on shoplifting. This new talent could come in handy.

She was beginning to suspect that the increase in business had less to do with Cupid Hollow's decreased number of shopping venues than she'd thought. The flurry of activity and excitement carried a supernatural tension. Could it be the cache of magic arrows? She pulled Gram aside. "Can you hold down the fort while I read those instructions and deal with Scott?"

"Of course, child." Gram patted her shoulder and bustled

off to open the cash register, so Val ducked into the office and found a slip of paper in one of the opened boxes of arrows and read it.

1. To create attraction or reverse effect of platinum* arrow use gold arrow.

2. To create animosity or reverse effect of gold arrow use platinum* arrow.

3. Effects last 2–3 days.

4. Keep away from all mortal-designed electronics. Manufacturer is not responsible for damage.

5. The use of this product has not been evaluated in children or adolescents.

* Pursuant to health and safety regulations regarding the safekeeping of mortals, lead content has been replaced by platinum.

Okay. So she had to find Scott at the high school and shoot him with a platinum arrow (it wouldn't cause lead poisoning—at least there was that to be thankful for) when as a non-student and a non-parent she had no valid reason to be there. She'd figure that out on the way.

She rushed as fast as she could to the opposite side of the office, tripped over the leg of the chair, and went sprawling. Her heart sank in her chest. The supernatural speed and agility had definitely not stuck with her. She picked herself up and looked inside the box that'd been opened. It contained both gold and platinum arrows, about ten gold ones for every platinum one. She carefully lifted out a platinum arrow then selected a spare to be on the safe side.

After securely locking the office door, she crept out the back exit. She tried not to dwell on the fact that she was stalking her best friend's fifteen-year-old son with Cupid's bow.

eight

As she exited the alley and emerged onto a side street, the air shimmered with glittering threads connecting the townspeople to each other. Then the sun broke through the clouds and the filigree vanished. Val blew out a breath and hurried onward, somewhat relieved not to see the threads. This errand was bizarre enough without special effects.

She approached the two-story brick high school. A man walking the other direction, his puffy parka hanging open over a garish Hawaiian-print shirt that strained to cover his round belly, nodded to her. She nodded back as she rushed past him. If she hurried, she'd be able to find Scott before classes began.

The school's bell clangored and kept ringing on and on. Seconds later students came pouring out the doors and down the front stairs, whipping out their cell phones and typing madly with their thumbs as they walked. It felt far too early for lunch. She pulled out her own phone to check the time, but the display was dark. She must've forgotten to charge it.

She scanned the melee but couldn't see Scott. The rising sun was in her eyes, and she stepped toward the school building to get into the shade so she could see better. And then all she could see was a web of glittering threads stretching out from the crowd of teens. As slipped her phone back into her purse, a wave of disorientation made her stumble back. The onrush of students parted around her as though she were a stone in a stream. She was suffocating in the tumult of their hormone-riddled adolescent angst. Her heart beat frantically, but she couldn't move, couldn't escape.

Gradually the sensation abated as the teenagers dispersed, and she gasped in deep breaths.

Sharp footsteps rang on the concrete behind her.

"Val? What are you doing here?"

She closed her eyes for a second then turned to greet Deb. Concern etched lines on her best friend's face. Gram's warning rang in her head, and she struggled for a response that would protect her secret without betraying their friendship.

"Gram mentioned she'd heard at the hair salon that Scott might need some extra support this morning," she lied, "so I'm guessing you got a call from the school?"

She suddenly understood the weight of guilt. It was the same as the weight of the bow and the two platinum arrows in her purse.

Deb touched a fingertip to one impeccably groomed eyebrow—her version of dragging her fingers through her hair in moments of distress. "They said he went berserk. Vandalized the entire front of the building."

Had Scott taken more of Cupid's arrows from her office? Had any of them scratched him? Had any of them scratched other students?

She trudged over to the front of the school. Her feet felt like bricks. Arching lines of faint chips in the bricks marked the front of the school in the shape of a heart. And in the center of the heart were an *S* and a slanting line that looked an awful lot like half a *V*. He must've been caught before he finished.

Her breath whooshed out. Thank the gods all he'd done was deface school property.

"It might be a good idea to put the archery lessons on

hold for a while." She hauled open the front door and held it for Deb.

They entered the foyer together, and the receptionist caught Deb's eye and waved her toward the principal's office. "You can go right in."

"He's never acted this way before," Deb whispered, dragging Val along with her. "Do you think it could be puberty? The divorce? It has to be the divorce. I knew it would be hard on him, but…"

They rounded the corner. Scott was slouched on one of the chairs outside the principal's office. The lighting wasn't the best, and the threads coming from mother and son formed a complex web. Scott shot up like a windmill, a familiar gleam in his eye. "Valentine. So you couldn't stay away from *this*." He grinned and posed his gawky body.

Deb's skin flushed, and even more worry lines creased her forehead. She grabbed her son by the ear. "Now listen here, mister. You are going to apologize to Val this minute."

"Really, Deb, he doesn't have to." Val kept talking, letting her words meander. While everyone's feelings ran high and their attention was distracted, she dipped her hands inside her purse and fitted an arrow into the bow, and raised its tip over the edge of the purse.

Ready.

"I'm sure this will all blow over by tomorrow."

"Valentine. Sweetheart." Scott's hand splayed theatrically over his heart. "I apologize for my mother's behavior."

Aim.

"No apology necessary."

Fire.

As the bow released, the door behind Scott opened.

Principal Laraine Street rubbed her shoulder then shot Scott a gaze filled with loathing. Oh. Crap.

"In my office," she barked at Scott. "Now."

Deb started toward the door, but Laraine held up her palm. She closeted herself in the office with Scott. Muted scolding ensued.

Val sank onto the chair and leaned her head against the wall. She waited for Deb to sit and then turned toward her. "I can explain what's going on."

She just wasn't sure how. Gram's warning rose in the back of her mind again. *Don't. Not ever, do you understand?*

"He confided in you?" The hurt on Deb's face was palpable. She and Scott had been extremely close until the divorce, and the new distance between them was something Val knew she still grieved deeply.

"No, not exactly. I just think I may have some insight into… this morning." She wasn't going to break her promise keeping the strange lines of light a secret. But Deb had been her best friend since they were in preschool and deserved to know the truth. At least, as much of it as Val could share. Val would tell her enough so she could understand what was happening to her son. It was Val's fault, after all. She opened her purse and tilted it so Deb could see the bow—and then she realized how stupid it was to expect Deb to accept that Val was for all intents and purposes a goddess. Look how much Val herself had resisted believing it. So she switched courses.

"It's a rare artifact—really rare to find it together with the little arrows. I was going to lock it all up—especially the arrows—in a display case today, because I've been researching it, and I suspect the arrow tips may have been coated with a chemical that temporarily affects—"

Deb softly banged the back of her head against the wall three times. "I am surrounded by lunacy."

"It only seems that way. I can undo this. There are two kinds of arrows—the second type reverses the effects of the first. Like an antidote. Luckily, both types were with the bow when it was found." That sounded unlikely even to Val. But not half as unlikely as the truth.

"You're going to experiment on my son with god only knows what kind of chemicals dug up from some hole in the ground?" Deb shook her head. "No. No, you won't. You're going to get up and walk out of this school, and you're going to stay away from my child."

"But it's my fault. I can help—"

"Don't make me get a restraining order," Deb said quietly.

Val got up. Her eyes burned, and her throat tried to close. "I'm sorry."

Deb closed her eyes. "Please don't talk to me."

She had to undo this. Had to. She nodded, though Deb's eyes were still shut. The thread of light between them had dimmed until it was barely there. If the threads were what she was beginning to suspect, a visible element of the emotional connection between two people, Val had all but destroyed the closest friendship she'd ever had.

Before leaving the school, she folded the remaining platinum arrow into a sheet of paper and wrote Scott's name on the outside. When no one was looking, she left it behind the reception counter and prayed he'd be clumsy enough to prick his finger a second time when he opened it.

She returned to her shop and worked with Gram, ringing up sales manually because the cash register was on the fritz. Her cell phone wouldn't take a charge, and the landline was down, so she had to call the repair guy from a pay phone down the street.

Vittorio hadn't dropped by, hadn't called, hadn't sent flowers. She began to wonder whether her judgment in men was a bit off. But the thread of light between them had been so strong and steady. If it weren't a nonstop marathon of customers in here, each person contributing to the mesh of light threads until she felt drawn in and trapped in their web, she'd be able to ask Gram about it again. But she had no opportunity to get Gram alone.

Worse, her guilt over what she'd let happen to Scott made her heart feel like Vittorio's entire stone temple was shattering inside her chest. Both events entirely her fault.

Just before three o'clock, she couldn't take it anymore. She ducked into the office, loaded her purse with arrows, and asked Gram to hold down the fort yet again. To be kind, she turned the sign in the door to Be Back Soon so Gram wouldn't be overwhelmed while she was gone. Then she headed straight for the high school. In the event Scott hadn't gotten the arrow she'd left him, she was going to undo the trouble she'd caused. She owed it to Scott—and especially to Deb.

Back at the school, she pretended to be out for a stroll. The bell rang, signaling the end of the school day, and the students flooded out. This time she kept more of a distance, and the tangle of teenage emotions didn't overcome her. Scott was among them. He glanced up at her, shrugged, took the hand of one of the girls, and continued on his way with his friends.

Val breathed a silent thanks.

She'd brought a newspaper with her, and when she saw Principal Street exit the building, she held the paper over her purse like a spy would, aimed, and fired. The gold arrow hit its target, and the tension drained visibly from the principal's shoulders.

None of the teens seemed to be behaving unusually.

Val sagged in relief—until she saw the man in the loudly colored shirt. He was the same guy she'd nodded to this morning, but this time he had his cell phone held up to capture both her and Laraine Street. He could only be taking a picture or recording video. When he noticed her watching him, he pocketed his phone and scuttled away.

Vittorio waited in an institutional-beige hallway, drumming his fingers on the arm of the deliberately uncomfortable chair. One would expect the deity division of the Canada Revenue Agency to have finer amenities than this, but apparently being a god didn't count for much when it came to taxes. Why in blazes couldn't you just cancel an audit by e-mail nowadays?

The shareholder meeting had gone badly. Timely land acquisition was important, and things in Cupid's Hollow weren't progressing as quickly as they should. Of course they weren't—not even a god could convince the progeny of Cupid to give up her property—and thus her soul and the powers that resided in it. And even if it could be done, it would be wrong. The law that assigned ownership of a soul alongside ownership of property had been put in place not to allow the possession of someone else's soul but to prevent the descendants of the gods from doing utterly moronic things like signing away their powers to another god.

Such a doubling up of god powers would be dangerous in the wrong hands. Like, say, the hands of Bacchus.

Had Vittorio known that Valentine was of Cupid's line— or the line of any god—he never would have made that bet. Never. So of course he held himself personally responsible for the added danger she was in due to the audit that he'd pulled strings in order to set in motion. She couldn't be distracted now. Not even a little. Her very soul was at stake. He had to undo the trouble he'd caused her.

A door across the hall opened, and a woman poked her head out and frowned at him. "You can come in now."

He followed her into a small, dingy office. It was the sort of room that would make its occupant grow miserable and vindictive over the years; he felt like snapping at the auditor after being in here for just a few moments.

She glanced down at a thick file lying open on her desk then smiled coolly at him. "I see your company, Jupitropolis, has taken an unusual interest in numerous businesses in Cupid's Hollow. Particularly Valentine Sports. Would you like to start by telling me why?"

Not really. Besides, if she didn't know why, she was patently unqualified for her job.

"It won't be necessary to run an audit on any of the businesses in Cupid's Hollow just because my company requested their accounts to be flagged. It was an interdepartmental miscommunication within Jupitropolis. I know how busy you are here"—he gestured to her overflowing file cabinets—"and I'm terribly sorry to have caused unnecessary work for you."

"I appreciate your coming in." She scribbled a note on a piece of paper and then placed it on the stack of records in the file on her desk. She delivered that cool-as-ice smile again. "But the audits have already begun, so there's no way to stop them."

Vittorio barely managed to rein in his anger before it could cause a surge of electricity that would destroy every electronic device in the CRA. "I'm sure there is a way."

These people could never be reasonable. He reached for his wallet, wondering what her price was.

"You did *not* just try to bribe an officer of the deity division of the Canada Revenue Agency." She poised her hand just under her desk. Was there a panic button under there? A bribery reporting button? "Did you?"

He sought a business card and extracted it from his wallet with his fingertips, leaving the wad of bills untouched. Offered the card to her. "Of course not. You may need to update my contact information."

When she didn't move to take the card, he dropped it on the file.

"Have a nice day." Then, because he had learned the hard way that no woman likes to be thought of as old or matronly, he added, "Ma'am."

The agent raised a brow at him and shooed him from her office. *Shooed* him. Shooed *him*.

He knocked back his chair and stormed out of the building, the *pop* of exploding light bulbs and startled exclamations following him.

He'd arranged for the audit only to distract and overwhelm a mortal woman so that he could swoop in and snatch up her property.

Gods. That made him sound exactly like the greedy corporate shark everyone said he was.

He needed to find a different way to build the new Jupitropolis store. A way that didn't involve Valentine Arciere losing her soul, even to him. The sheer impossibility of that task made him bow his head and clamp his palms over his temples.

Finally five o'clock came, and Val locked the shop's front door and turned the sign to Closed while Gram hustled to the back of the store for one last Facebook fix.

A high-pitched beeping sound emanated from the office.

"Sweetheart?" Gram called. "Something's wrong with this blasted computer."

Val sighed and went to see what was up. Instead of Gram's Facebook page, the monitor showed a blank slate of blue. The beeping was grating on her nerves. "Did you try restarting it?"

Gram reached for the power button, and Val had time to notice the soft glow of the thread connecting them. It was unlike the other threads she'd been seeing, but when she tried to describe it to herself, the only thing she could come up with was that it looked like loyalty and devotion. Maybe the threads were more than just the emotional connections between people. Maybe they also revealed a person's character. She recalled getting the sense that nobody in the lineup in front of the store this morning was a shoplifter. Her sensing of the complexity of the threads had grown more distinct by the hour, and part of her wished she could escape this unwilling invasion of people's privacy. It was like being bombarded by a never-ending stream of sound bites until she was ready to scream just to drown it out.

Before Gram's finger touched the computer's power button, the machine fell silent.

Then the screen went black.

No combination of pressing and holding the power button, fiddling with the cord and battery, and tapping the side of the computer would convince it to reboot. Val picked up the phone. Still dead. She eyed the stack of hand-written sales receipts that would have to be entered into the system. There was no way they could continue to do business without a functioning computer. She found a piece of cardboard and a Sharpie and made a sign to put in the door to let customers know they'd be closed for a day or two due to an equipment failure. Thank the gods she backed up the shop's data daily on a thumb drive she kept in her purse.

"Let's call it a day," she suggested. "I'll order a new computer, put the data on it, enter today's sales, and we'll be up and running again by the end of the week." It could've been much sooner than that if Cupid's Hollow had a Jupitropolis. She groaned to herself. "On second thought, I bet John Jones can do something with it. Just because he sold his store doesn't mean he forgot how to fix computers."

She tried to keep Vittorio off her mind as she called John's home number and arranged to drop off the computer that evening.

Had she been just a one-night stand to him? She traced

the filament of light that stretched from her chest to... wherever he was. Maybe she didn't know what it was after all.

"I almost forgot." Gram picked up an official-looking envelope from the desk and handed it to her. The flap had been cut, and the contents peeped out.

"What's this?" Val frowned at the return address, which contained the words *Canada Revenue Agency.*

"We're being audited," Gram informed her gravely.

"Oh, good." She rolled her eyes. A dead computer *and* an audit. Who needed sleep anyway?

Eying the boxes of arrows, she handed Gram her car keys. "Would you mind opening the trunk? I'm going to take these things home where they can't cause any more trouble."

nine

*J*OHN JONES WAS out behind his house chopping fire-wood when Val arrived to drop off her computer; she found him by following the *thunk, thunk* of the ax.

He hefted the ax and thumped it down, embedding the edge of the blade in the chopping block, then wiped his hands on his faded jeans and turned to face her. His cheeks were gaunt and unshaven, and as his gaze took in her lamé bag and leather pants, a sad look flitted across his face. The threads of light coming from him were more slender than any she'd seen, their glow feeble compared with the strength of the ones that bound her to Gram—and, she noted, to Vittorio. She hoped tonight he would make good on his promise to call her.

"You still holding out, eh?" John rubbed his whiskers. When had he gone so gray? "Good for you, I guess."

She wished she'd taken the time to change into some regular clothes after she dropped Gram off at home. John didn't look like he was doing so well—financially or otherwise—and she didn't want to make things worse for him by showing up looking like she'd come from some exclusive boutique in Vancouver. Besides, what she wore today wasn't really her. She was regular folks, just like everyone in Cupid's Hollow. Except... she wasn't, really. Not after last night. She swallowed.

"You don't mind taking a look at my computer?"

Slowly, he nodded. "You brought it?"

"It's in the car. I'll go get it."

But he'd already stridden past her, and he got to the car ahead of her and lifted her computer from the backseat. "I'll get started tonight. Never know, it might be something quick, get you back up and running for tomorrow."

It gave her a twisting sensation inside that a man as nice as John, so hardworking and thoughtful, seemed to be in such a bad place in the shadow of the situation with Jupitropolis, while she was the one holding out against the megacorporation, and she wasn't suffering in the least.

Of course, he'd accepted a payout from Jupitropolis of his own free will, just like every other shop owner on Main Street had—and payouts like that weren't exactly a pittance. She'd been offered a nice sum for Valentine Sports. More than nice. Enough to keep her afloat for years and then some, if she'd accepted it.

Maybe he always wore ratty clothes at home; he was doing chores, after all. Maybe his grizzled stubble was a personal style choice. Maybe his overly thin face and sunken eyes were none of her business.

She shouldn't pry. But…

"John." She laid a hand on his sleeve. "Is everything okay?"

He glanced at her sadly. "Nothing I can do anything about, so I just take one day at a time. I'll let you know about the computer, Val. And you give my best to Maria."

It felt as though he was rushing her away, and obviously he was telling her it was none of her business, so she nodded and said thanks and then got into her car and drove home. Full darkness had fallen over Cupid's hollow, and traces of light laid a faint glimmer over the streets. The entire town glowed in an interconnected web of relationships. She found it oddly comforting, the way her own light and Gram's mingled with everyone else's.

And there was one other ray of sunshine in an otherwise cloudy day. She patted her purse. Thank the gods she had that backup of all her data on the memory stick, or she'd be in real trouble when the day for the audit arrived.

Now that she had a moment to think about that particular upcoming day of fun and games, she decided it would be better to go through the extra trouble of installing her bookkeeping software on her laptop at home. Tonight. Just in case. Then if John could save the store computer by tomorrow, fine, she'd have wasted a little of her own time; but if the computer were terminally ill, she'd use her laptop at the store until after the audit.

She couldn't get the look on John's face out of her mind. He obviously blamed her for the shutdown of every business on Main Street other than hers. Maybe he was right. Maybe she *should* sell out to Jupitropolis.

At a red light, she peeked at her cell phone to check for missed calls, hoping to see Vittorio's name on the Caller ID. But the silly battery was still dead.

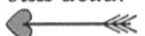

"Gram," Val called as she packed a box of arrows in from the car, "Did anyone call for me while I was out?"

"In here, dear. Can you see if you can do something with this dratted contraption?"

She set the box in the hall and poked her head into the living room, where Gram was peering at the power cord for Val's laptop. "What's up?"

Gram shook the end of the cord then plugged it extra firmly into the back of the laptop. "I printed out some important e-mails, and then it just went to sleep. I can't wake it up. I think it's dead," she pronounced solemnly, blinking owlishly through her bifocals.

Val's stomach did a loop. "I hope not."

Normally she'd remind Gram she didn't need to print out

every single thing, but with two computer problems in one day, maybe Gram's printing addiction wasn't such a bad thing.

She checked the electrical connection, tried a different outlet, made sure the battery was installed correctly. The machine refused to do so much as light up even one tiny little LED.

"Well." She flopped onto the couch beside Gram. "No Facebook for you tonight, I guess." And no being prepared for that audit, either.

"That's not funny."

It was, actually, because Gram could pout with the best of them. Val tried hard not to laugh, and she mostly succeeded.

The landline rang, and she jumped up, pulse fluttering. *Vittorio.* But the Caller ID said otherwise. She forced herself not to sound as disappointed as she felt. "Maybe John has good news."

After a short, extremely disappointing conversation, Val let the phone receiver drop back to its cradle. She breathed in a deliberately calm manner, hoping that would help her actually feel some of the peace she was in short supply of.

It didn't really help.

"John said the shop computer is—and I quote—hooped. Because all the components are fried. He said that's the technical term for it."

"That's not good, I take it?" The scrunch of Gram's face spoke her alarm. Behind those innocent blue eyes, you could practically see the Facebook withdrawal symptoms starting.

Val shook her head. "I'll have to order a new computer after all." It wouldn't leave much time to prepare for the audit, but what else could she do? Unless... "Gram, you didn't happen to print out our year-end reports, did you?"

"I *would* have, but you wanted to wait until the printer paper was on sale," Gram said indignantly.

Of course. Why shouldn't a perfectly sensible decision come back to bite her in the butt?

"Okay, don't worry about it. I'll sort things out after I put the data onto the new computer."

Gram said she was going to hit the hay, so Val plugged her cell phone into the charger she kept at home—she'd have to take this one to work, since the one at the store hadn't charged the phone today—and then wandered over to the printer to see what e-mail had been so important.

It was one page. A receipt for an eBay purchase of miniature arrows—with a total exceeding ten thousand dollars. A whimper crawled from her throat. Her leg bones turned into cooked spaghetti, and she grabbed the wall so she wouldn't topple over. *Oh, Gram. What did you do now?* At the bottom of the receipt, in large bold print:

No refunds. No exchanges. All sales final.

It felt as though her heart had gotten lodged in her throat. Or a basketball, maybe. The three-thirty wakeup call from the police still rang in her ears. *Your store was vandalized. You should get down there and secure the premises.*

When she parked outside the shop, all she could do at first was sit in her car and stare into the dim interior of Valentine Sports.

The shop was between street lights and not very well illuminated. Bright crescents of moonlight glinted from shards of broken glass strewn across the sidewalk, tangling with the faint web of glittering threads that overlaid the town. She slowly got out of the car. The display of figure skates in the window was destroyed. Ski gloves and toques had been strewn over the floor. Clothing racks had been upended, the athletic wear that had been hanging neatly on them tossed about like clothing in a teenager's bedroom.

The place looked like a—like a crime scene.

She let out a sharp sob. Her beautiful store. Who would do this to her? Why?

It hurt so much. She wished Gram were here, she'd know what to do. But this store was Gram's, too, and it would break her heart to see it like this. Step by step, her boots crunching broken glass, she approached the door.

Out of habit, she put her key in the lock of the door, and then she laughed bitterly. Who needed a key when she could walk right through the empty door frame?

She didn't have any way to board up the front of the store until later in the morning when the building stores would open, but she should at least find a broom and sweep up the glass.

Stumbling over the wreckage, she made her way to the counter, where the light switch was located, and turned on the overhead lights.

That only made it worse.

Across the length of one entire wall, someone had spray painted in dripping red letters an echo of another warning she'd been given. "SELL OR YOU'LL BE SORRY."

Feeling sick, she pressed her palm over her mouth. Was standing up for what she believed in so offensive that someone would deliberately destroy her store? It seemed so.

Gradually she realized a notice of some sort had been nailed to the wall below the warning. She picked her way closer to it, clambering around a toppled rack of ski poles that looked like a giant game of pick-up-sticks, and pulled it from the nail. It was a copy of the offer from Jupitropolis. At the bottom of the paper, highlighted in bright yellow, she read, "Moneys to be paid out after commencement of construction of the Cupid's Hollow Jupitropolis megastore."

That didn't make any sense. Who would even agree to something like that?

She recalled John Jones's sad eyes. He'd signed it. And so

had the owners of all the businesses along the dark, empty Main Street. Everybody except her. She hadn't actually bothered to read the entire contract Jupitropolis had offered, because she'd never for a moment considered selling out to the huge corporation.

She swallowed. Her business, the town she'd grown up in, the people she'd known all her life… all of it could be destroyed if she didn't bow to the will of the mighty Jupitropolis. Jupiter. The king of gods. Her pulse hammered slow and hard.

At the helm of that corporation could well be the descendant of the king of gods, Vittorio Fulminare.

The others must feel like she was the bad guy here. And wasn't she? Standing her ground, standing up for what she believed in, while everyone around her suffered because of her actions.

"Mom… Dad," she whispered, crumpling to her knees. "I don't know what to do."

Her boot brushed against something that tinkled. Her brass bell, lying on the floor amid the ruins of her dreams. She stretched out her fingers to pick up the bell, but then she let her hand fall to her side. Slowly she got to her feet and walked back out onto the dark street.

Bacchus lifted the enchantment from the Quintarelli so he could properly enjoy it; it was never quite as exquisite when it was disguised as beer. He took a long sip and groaned with pleasure. Less from the wine than from the knowledge of what he held in his hand.

He hadn't expected to win either bet fairly. It seemed almost too easy, especially after the spawn of lusty old Cupid had so blindly tumbled into Jupiter's bed. Her turning out not to be mortal should have cemented the more important bet for him—after all, every other business owner in this backwater town had rolled over with barely a whimper, and she was still holding out. How lucky could a god get? However, Bacchus wasn't one to leave anything to chance. Least of all the acquisition of a soul.

The envelope had been delivered moments after Jupiter stepped into the shower. The idiot king was wallowing in there still, bellowing some off-key love song. Bacchus shuddered. Well. Let him have his moment. Because the Consortium of gods had called an emergency meeting about the situation in Cupid's Hollow (thanks to Bacchus, actually), and yours truly was going to make certain the arrogant prick didn't show up.

He held a lighter to the corner of the summons. The flame licked at the parchment. He waited for it to catch.

But it didn't. He ground his molars so hard the coffeepot rattled on its hotplate. A failsafe. So much for it being too easy.

There was still a way, though. If he couldn't destroy the summons, all he had to do was ensure the idiot king didn't find it.

The water in the bathroom stopped running.

Bacchus moved fast, the tails of his Hawaiian shirt flapping.

As the bathroom door swung open and steam billowed out, he lolled in the room's dreadfully uncomfortable chair... and *Brandon* let out a raucous belch and raised his glass of cheap beer in a toast to Vittorio.

ten

WALKING INTO THE library with Gram this morning, Val could feel the accusation in the other patrons' stares. Everyone she knew blamed her for the slow death of Main Street. She tried not to wonder which of them might be responsible for the much swifter destruction of her shop. Gram toddled off to a computer for her Facebook fix, and Val slipped into a seat at the next machine. She went to the Staples website and ordered a replacement computer for the shop—which officially maxed out her credit—and then went to stand at the window while she waited for Gram to finish. The library was on a bit of a rise, a few blocks away from Valentine Sports. She could see a bustle of activity there already; the insurance company had sent a contractor to board up the gaping holes where the big display window and the door had been.

A sleek, familiar car crawled to a stop in front of the shop. It sat there for a few moments and then surged forward. Vittorio. Her breath caught. He'd come looking for her, and she wasn't there. Would he be worried for her safety? She didn't even know his cell phone number, so she couldn't run to a phone and tell him she was all right.

Whoa. They'd spent one—albeit glorious—night together, and he hadn't even called her afterward, and she was sending herself into a flap because he *might* be worried about her? Well, *she* was worried about her. Her business might be in a hole so deep she could never dig it out, thanks to Gram and her eBay addiction. And everyone she knew, except Gram, had every right to hate her.

Even in the sun, she thought she could detect a faintly glimmering thread that wended its way between her and Vittorio. Slowly, deliberately, she turned away and slid back into the seat beside Gram's.

"I think maybe I should sell," she said quietly.

Gram didn't seem to hear her. Then she pushed away the mouse and turned to face Val. She took her hands and squeezed them harder than an old lady should be able to, so hard it hurt. "You must *never* sell," she whispered fiercely.

"I can't do this anymore." Val bit the side of her lower lip. "What good is holding up an ideal if all I'm doing is hurting everyone I know?"

"There are things you don't know about being a goddess, and we're not discussing them here." Gram blinked. Val was starting to wonder if those new bifocals were mortal in origin—they gave Gram's stare a palpable physical effect on her, and she shivered.

"I think it's high time we *did* discuss those things."

"Val." There was something about the way the king of gods said her name that made it just about impossible for her to stay in her chair. Somehow she did, though she wanted nothing more than to jump up and throw herself into his arms and demand they go somewhere very private for a very long time. Though she had managed to control her legs, she wasn't able to stop the hot blush from racing up her neck to her face. He touched her cheek. "I couldn't reach you on your phone, so when I saw your car here, I—I'm relieved to see you're all right."

But she wasn't all right. Since Jupitropolis decided to take over her town, nothing had been *all right*. She carefully stood, keeping a couple of feet of space between them. Part of her mind registered a man standing behind him, a stout man wearing a garish Hawaiian shirt. He looked vaguely familiar, and as she tried to place where she'd seen him, he turned to gaze at Deb, who'd just walked in and flashed him a brilliant smile. Which was odd, because Deb had higher standards than that. But Val had other things on her mind right now.

"Vittorio, we need to talk."

His eyelids hooded his eyes. "Perhaps not here," he suggested.

"Actually, yes. Here." Because if they weren't where people could see them, their conversation wouldn't end in anything but lovemaking. Gratifying as that would be, it wouldn't solve the issue of Vittorio's probably being the man behind the corporation that was threatening to eat up Cupid's Hollow. She made sure to keep her voice low, though. No sense in anyone realizing this was anything more than a mere mortal conversation. "I have a question, and I need you to answer it truthfully."

"I could not do otherwise, amore mio."

A radiance made her glance downward. The thread of light that bound them together had grown as thick and strong as one of the pillars of Jupiter's temple, and it was glowing so brightly, it lit up Vittorio's face. How could nobody else see it? She wondered whether the connection between them would crumble as the temple itself had, leaving only rubble and dust to mark its passing.

Val forced herself to ask the question whose answer she needed but desperately didn't want to hear. "Are you the head of Jupitropolis?"

She could feel the tension flowing from him. She knew what he was going to say, and she wished she wouldn't have asked, because anything except no would be a deal breaker. It had to be. She couldn't be involved with a man who was bent on destroying the dreams of her community, the dreams of her parents. A muscle in his cheek twitched. "Yes."

Her heart, her world, dropped in a sickening freefall. "Then you're responsible for everyone I know and love and respect losing their businesses."

"Yes." He looked uncomfortable.

"And you're not going to stop until I sell out, too."

"Valentine, please understand."

"Just answer." Her throat ached with the effort of holding back a sob.

"Yes."

"Then"—her world was coming apart, crashing around her in choking clouds of dust—"I can't be with you anymore."

"Bella, no. Let us talk." His voice cracked, raw and hoarse.

Overhead, a fluorescent tube popped and went dark. The rest of the lights extinguished themselves, and the only sound was the fading whine of computers. The library fell into darkness.

"Just go," she whispered. She closed her eyes. "Please."

She could feel the trace of his finger along her cheekbone, and his touch felt so right, hot tears slipped between her lashes.

When she opened her eyes, he was gone.

Gram's gentle hand settled on her shoulder. "I know your pain, little one. But you couldn't have chosen otherwise."

Val wrenched herself away and stared out the window, tears rolling down her face as she watched Vittorio's car roar away from the curb. Nothing had felt like a *choice* since she'd met him—since Gram had shot her with that first stupid arrow.

Val slumped on the couch, watching the angle of the sun change by degrees. She'd been moping around the house for days, clad in her pajamas, without even the energy to drag herself into the shower. It was probably the massive quantity of chocolate she'd been consoling herself with, but she couldn't bring herself to care that overnight she'd let herself go from goddess of love to housebound slob.

Sure, technically she'd been the one to tell Vittorio she couldn't be with him anymore.

But the jerk had agreed! He hadn't tried to contact her even once.

And now here she was, having faced the Purolator delivery guy looking like she hadn't showered in a week—which was roughly accurate—and with little to no hope of entering all her data into the new computer before the auditor arrived.

The one time she did venture out into the cold and the snow and the wind, to check with the police about the investigation into the break-in at her shop, she'd learned there was no hope of catching the culprit. He'd left no prints, no trace of himself other than the havoc he'd wreaked. And just like her computer and her cell phone, all the surveillance cameras on Main Street had malfunctioned.

She groaned. And she smelled bad. Even Gram, who normally was pretty easy-going, had made some barely disguised noises of disapproval when Val raised her arm to get a glass from the kitchen cabinet this morning. Maybe if she took a shower, she'd feel more like facing the day.

She trudged to the bathroom, dropped her pajamas on the floor, and stood under the hot water for a good long while, willing it to melt away her lethargy along with the layer of grime and sweat she'd accumulated like a sloth accumulated moss. Eventually the water grew cold and she had to get out.

Clean clothes were folded neatly over the towel rack, and her nasty jammies had disappeared. She bit back a smile at Gram's unique brand of logic—no chance of Val slipping back into her stupor of depression if her crusty pajamas were unavailable.

And the shower did help a little. She actually felt like she could manage to do some data entry and even face the auditor. And then, as soon as all this was over, she was going to sign the buy-out contract. No matter how Gram felt, the store was just a store, and she'd assigned far too much meaning to it. It had taken over her entire life to the point where she was willing to sacrifice her community for it. Well, no more. Cupid's Hollow would get its Jupitropolis. And as for Val—well, she was a resourceful woman, and she'd set up shop somewhere else. Maybe even use the buy-out money to build a bigger indoor range that wasn't in a basement.

Her heart didn't feel quite so heavy as she fetched the USB stick from her purse and carried the new computer to the kitchen and got it booted up. She'd had the foresight to pay extra for the operating system to be installed and ready to go, so the only thing she had to do before backing up her bookkeeping data and entering in that last day of records was install QuickBooks. She turned on the computer.

Gram was puttering around and laid a hand on Val's shoulder as she walked by. "Welcome back, little one."

That was it. No judgment, just… acceptance.

Val slipped a disk into the drive and clicked the appropriate buttons. "Gram, now that I smell better, can we talk about all the mysterious *stuff*?"

"Mm." Gram gazed wistfully at the computer screen, probably suffering from near-terminal social networking anxiety. "That would be a good idea. Where do you want to start, child?"

Did it matter? Nothing about this new existence made any sense. The accounting software requested her to insert another disk, and that decided the topic: implications of deity on business.

"How about with why you think it's such a bad idea to sell the store?"

"Why not start with something difficult?" Gram muttered. She wandered back out of the kitchen for several minutes and came back with a piece of stiff, yellowed paper. Huffing a deep sigh, she poured Val a big cup of coffee and sat at the table with her. "Our family is tied to the property the store sits on."

"Most people have an attachment for things they own." Val sipped the strong, dark coffee. It was a nice change from the sweet chocolate she'd been filling her face with all week.

"Mortal souls change hands as often as a real estate deal is signed. It's as inconsequential as a game of go fish. But it's different for us." She pushed the paper across the table to Val. "Read this."

The writing was in Latin. Or Italian. Either way, it was Greek to Val. "I must've been away the day they taught the other Romance languages in French class, Gram."

There was that owlish blink again. "They don't teach young people anything important in school anymore. Well. Here's the gist of it, then."

Val listened, horrified, as Gram explained that should Val sell the store, the buyer would come into possession of not just the sports shop but also of…

Val's soul.

"Holy crap, Gram!" She choked on her coffee. "That's the kind of thing you need to tell a person. What if I'd accepted the offer from Jupitropolis?"

Gram snorted. "You wouldn't have done that."

She'd come so close to it, though. Nice of Vittorio to let her know the consequences of it, too. "Maybe. Uh. Maybe… okay, then. No selling the store. Got it."

She remembered Deb complaining that she was surrounded by lunacy. Deb didn't know the half of it. It occurred to Val that she herself *did* know the half of it—and the other half had to do with the threads of light she kept seeing.

"Now, about the light connecting us."

The computer prompted her to click something. She attended to the installation of the software then turned her attention back to Gram.

"Yes." Gram gulped her coffee but didn't offer an explanation.

"It's unusual that I see it," Val prompted.

"Yes."

"Gram!"

"Well…"

"Hang on." The installation was complete. Val inserted the thumb drive. A window popped up showing its contents. Which were… gone. All the air seeped from her lungs. Frantically she pulled out the little device, blew imaginary crumbs from the connections, and plugged it into a different port. Empty. All her data, years of invoices and purchase orders and vendor listings and year-end reports, and the auditor was going to make sure she went to jail for the rest of her natural life. It took all the concentration she possessed simply to take the next breath.

How could this have happened? She'd faithfully backed everything up, always kept the thumb drive in her purse, always kept her purse away from magnets, stereo speakers, anything that could damage electronics. Nothing about that had changed since—the arrows. Ever since the arrows had arrived in the store, the electronics had been going wonky. And she'd been carrying them around in her purse. Val whimpered.

"And that's why you must *never* tell anyone you can see the threads," Gram pronounced.

"Sorry, Gram." Gone. All gone. How was she going to get through the audit? "Could you repeat—"

A polite *tap-tap* sounded from the door.

Val got up from the table and went to answer the door.

An official-looking woman with a briefcase stood on the front step. She didn't smile or offer her hand. "I'm Sara, with Canada Revenue. I assume you're ready for your audit."

Gram puttered in from the kitchen. "I knew there was *something* I forgot to tell you, Val. We've been... ah... rescheduled."

eleven

GRAM EXCUSED HERSELF, saying she was exhausted and needed to rest—leaving Val at the mercy of the auditor, whom she led to the kitchen so the agent could see for herself what was going on with the computer situation.

"What are the chances we could reschedule?" Judging by Sara's shark eyes, slim to none.

After briefly consulting a day planner, Sara snapped it closed. "That won't be possible. Let's get started."

"I'll get everything I have, but it's not much." Val explained about the computer failure and the loss of her data, knowing how evasive she sounded, but it was the truth. With each sentence out of her mouth, she could see the annoyance building in Sara's face. And when she produced her stack of receipts—the totality of her business records—the auditor looked in serious danger of the top of her head blowing completely off from sheer anger.

"I've never seen such—you're simply—blatant dishonesty!" Twin spots of red glared on her cheeks. "I don't know what you're trying to hide, but I promise you, I intend to get to the bottom of… oh."

Her expression softened.

Had that been a tiny flash of gold Val saw streaking across the room? She glanced over Sara's shoulder and spotted Gram dropping the bow back into her purse and then scuttling off to her bedroom.

Sara sidled closer to Val. "You know, there may be something I can do to help." She ran her tongue across her lower lip.

Was the auditor coming on to her?

"I… ah… maybe we can talk about this another time," Val suggested, backing away.

Sara darted after her and brushed a strand of hair from Val's face. Her breath smelled like Listerine, clinical and no-nonsense. "I can definitely help you."

"Gram," Val shouted. "Gram, we need to talk about something right now!"

She heard the faint *click* of Gram's bedroom door locking. The little sneak.

"Looks like it's just you and me." The auditor, who had a remarkable talent for noticing the obvious, had somehow backed her against the kitchen cabinets. She planted a hand on the counter on either side of Val, bracketing her hips with her arms. She leaned close, her mouthwash breath wafting across Val's face with the promise of a bookkeepingly good time.

Val didn't see any choice but to—

Duck under the love-struck auditor's arm and make a mad dash for her purse. Working as quickly as humanly possible—and to her bone-deep relief, she could sense her hands moving with a speed beyond purely human—she fitted a platinum bolt into Cupid's bow. She snatched up an afghan from the couch to conceal the weapon. Turned to face her foe.

Sara was charging across the room, a lustful gleam in her eye. "Lover," she purred, "come to mama."

Val squeezed the trigger. The tiny bolt streaked forward and found its mark the instant before Sara collided into her with a surprised grunt.

Glasses askew, cheeks flushed, Sara straightened her

jacket. She studied Val thoughtfully. "Maybe... we could re-schedule after all."

"Thank you." Had she just used her supernatural powers to evade dealing with her taxes? What kind of person *was* she? Not that she let her guilt over that stop her from showing Sara to the door.

With the audit put off for the moment, she let Gram know it was safe to come out. There was something odd about Sara, she thought, watching the woman walk dreamily to her station wagon and drive away. And then it hit her. The thread of light trailing behind the car was different from the others she'd seen. It was cold looking. Fractured.

"Gram." She beckoned her over and pointed.

But Gram shook her head. "I can't see them, child. Very few can."

"When you were telling me about them earlier, I'm sorry, it was right when I was having problems with the computer, and I didn't quite... tune in."

Gram sighed loudly. "Kids."

"Gram. I said I was sorry. I'm listening now."

With a skeptical glance, Gram seemed to decide she *was* listening this time. "It's a rare ability you have, little one. It hasn't been seen for generations, except in"—her eyes watered, but she forged on bravely—"your mother."

"Mom could see them too?" Why had everyone kept this a secret from her? This was something her parents should have shared with her, taught her how to deal with it instead of just tossing her to the wolves and expecting her to bumble through the bizarre world of gods and goddesses and superpowers on her own.

"She could. The Consortium of gods found out and wanted to exploit her ability to sense the very essence of people's emotions, their intent. Using her talent to enable the Consortium to have the upper hand in their business dealings would have given them an obscenely unfair advantage. She wouldn't agree." Gram's mouth tightened into a circle of little wrinkles. "And that's why they sank *Salacia*."

"They—they killed my parents?" Val's world contracted around her. There wasn't enough air. She didn't want this strange new life, the trickery, the lies, the danger.

"They did." Gram's voice was steady, her jaw set firm. "And you must *never* let on that you see those threads, child. Do you understand me?"

Val pressed her lips together. "I understand."

Bacchus backed away from the window where he'd been eavesdropping. His excursion to Cupid's Hollow was turning out to be more rewarding than he'd expected.

The daughter had inherited the sight. It was almost too good to be true.

As he slipped away through the shadows, he chuckled to himself. A little chat with his favorite CRA agent, a dab of creative contract wording, and by this time next week, he wouldn't need the idiot king for anything. By this time next week, Bacchus himself would be in possession of Valentine Sports—and with it the soul of the one who could see into the heart of each and every opponent he might want to topple.

But still. Perhaps he might run an errand before returning to the sordid little hotel where the idiot king was moping and gnashing his teeth. He'd been meaning to collect on a favor from Mercury for some time now. Yes. Yes, indeed. Tonight the god of revelry would have a little *incontro a due* with the god of travel.

The courier tapping his toe in front of Val was starting to make her feel nervous—as if the call from Sara the CRA auditor, via a messenger sent to her house with a cell phone (Val had to wait on hold for a full ninety minutes, too), hadn't stressed her out enough. She had a stack of official paperwork to sign and get back to the auditor this very day or risk having all her assets seized until after the audit was completed. She'd never heard of such a thing, but Sara had mentioned on the phone that she worked with the deity division. They must have different rules there. They certainly had different stationery—if you held it at an angle to the light, you could see a watermark in the shape of a complex crest bearing the words *deity division*.

One thing she had to be thankful for: the platinum arrow she'd shot the auditor with seemed to have fully canceled out the effects of the gold arrow Gram had shot her with, because Sara had been in fine, no-nonsense auditor form once again. Val would rather that than to have a complete stranger panting after her, which had made her uncomfortable to say the least.

Vittorio must have some kind of immunity to the arrows, since he hadn't tried to call her even once after she told him she didn't want to see him anymore. How could she have been so stupid as to fall into bed with the first god she met?

She scribbled her name across the line at the bottom of each page; her agreement that she wouldn't attempt to hide assets, wouldn't leave the country anytime soon, wouldn't do this, wouldn't do that.

If he didn't stop that tapping, she was going to scream. She paused and glared at him. "Do you mind?"

A sheepish look came over his face. "I'm sorry to make you rush, miss. It's just that if I don't get these papers back to the CRA today, I'll lose my job. It's kind of my last chance."

Now that was encouraging, wasn't it? Val put her name to the last of the forms. She hoped he couldn't read upside down, or he'd know the humiliating and terrifying truth— that she and Gram could lose their house, lose the store... be put out on the street in the cold of February.

She capped the pen and returned it to him with the stack of papers.

"Thank you." He bobbed his head and backed away, slipping the pages into a sturdy folder.

One fell out, and they both bent to pick it up at the same time. Their heads knocked together hard, and while they were reeling from the collision, Val got to the paper before the icy wind could snatch it away. When she went to hand it to him, her eyes watering with pain, a second sheet slid out from under the first.

It, too, had a line for her to sign.

The young man's eyes bulged. "Oh, man. Thank the gods you didn't miss that one. I'd have lost my job for sure."

"Yeah." She signed it and gave it back to him, watching to make sure it got safely into the folder with the others. "Thank the gods."

"I mean it, you really saved my bacon."

He left then, and Val went in and closed the door. Despite the warmth of the house, she couldn't shake the chill that had set in. He'd *better* get those papers delivered on time. Her assets depended on it.

Gram wandered into the living room, carrying two fur coats. "Which one of these do you think I should wear to the gala?"

Torn between two disparate worlds, Val couldn't come up with an opinion right away. "I'm not sure I feel up to going out, Gram."

"Nonsense. A good party is just what you need to take your mind off things. Besides, I'll bet your handsome young man will be expecting you."

Sometimes Gram could be deliberately obtuse. Like now. Val didn't like the devious glint in her eye. Not at all. "Vittorio and I aren't exactly an item. He's the head of Jupitropolis, remember? I'm not dating him."

"Pshaw." Gram batted her hand as though knocking aside any words she didn't agree with. "Don't you think I know a little bit about love, child? I do share your heritage."

That, Val hadn't considered until now. Actually, given what had happened at Jupiter's temple, she would really rather never think about Gram's heritage at all, because it was a hard picture to get out of her head.

"It doesn't matter," she said wearily. "Vittorio and I don't share the same values. We could never make a relationship work."

"As you wish." Gram rubbed one of the coats—rabbit, Val thought—against her cheek. "But I'm going to the gala to help my community celebrate the one thing big business can't take away—love—and since my lovely granddaughter refuses to kiss and make up with the best thing that's ever happened to her, she is going as *my* date."

"You're impossible," Val grumbled.

Gram flounced back to her room, humming loudly enough to drown out any protest Val could make.

Vittorio raced through the quaint hotel, sidestepping to avoid other guests. The summons hadn't said specifically what would be addressed at the emergency meeting of the Consortium, but the Consortium didn't call emergency meetings for inconsequential matters.

He could slap himself for failing to adequately supervise Randy. To mortal eyes, the summons would've looked like a flyer or some other meaningless piece of paper—and so it had been discarded. It wasn't Randy's fault. He couldn't possibly have known.

He checked the time. If he hurried, he'd get to the meeting before it was over.

The sleek black car awaited him at the curb. Though conscious of the seconds ticking past—and the startled bystanders—he approached the driver's-side door in a full-on sprint. For appearance's sake, he pulled out the key fob as he skidded to a halt and pretended he was unlocking the car. He slid his fingers into the door handle so it wouldn't look like it was opening itself.

The door remained closed.

He tugged at it, his pulse throbbing in his temples.

It wouldn't budge. What was wrong with the confounded thing?

Pasting on a befuddled grin, he pulled out his freshly charged cell phone. It looked like any mortal's cell phone but had been specially designed to stand up to the effects of his electric personality. He placed the call.

Seconds streamed by. Too many. Too fast.

The call connected. Vittorio cupped his hand around the phone and his mouth to prevent anyone from overhearing the conversation.

"Mercury, come to my location immediately. The car—"

"Sorry, to miss your call," a recorded voice answered. "Emergency meeting of the Consortium. Leave a message, and I'll call you back."

What good was the god of travel if he was going to be unavailable when you needed to travel?

Vittorio had enough time to either pull out fistfuls of his hair or…

Clutching the phone tightly, he gave the rear side window a sharp rap.

The phone shattered. So did the window.

Heads all over the street swiveled to watch him. Cell phones came out, the onlookers' fingers already dialing 911.

"It's all right," he shouted, dangling the remote opener for them to see. "Little battery problem, that's all."

He raised one hand in a wave as he reached into the car with his other hand to unlock the driver's door. Mustering a confident expression, he climbed in and inserted the key into the ignition.

The car started. Thank the gods.

He dropped his foot onto the accelerator.

Red-and-blue lights flashed in the mirrors.

Normally Vittorio was a law-abiding god—being responsible for overseeing such things. Right now he needed to make an exception. He urged the car to maximum speed and jumped the continuum between mortal and immortal worlds, leaving the policeman far behind.

He would apologize to himself later for breaking the law.

twelve

BACCHUS PATTED THE pocket of his suit jacket to make certain he still had the contents, then he checked that his Hawaiian-print tie was straight. The modern Consortium was much stodgier than it had been in the old times, and he knew better than to ruffle any feathers by violating the dress code too much. Look what had happened to the Arcieres when they didn't cooperate, after all. Even the bright print of his tie may be pushing it a little, but a fellow had to wear *something* showy. He licked his thumb and smoothed his eyebrows. Took one bracing sip from the flask he kept in another pocket.

All right, then. He was ready to do this thing.

He exited the magic conveyance into the bright Mediterranean sun. His footsteps rang out against the marble stairs leading up through soaring columns to the grand hall where the Consortium awaited his presence. As he entered the hall, lesser gods silently closed the doors behind him, sealing the chamber until the deed was finished. Every greater god but Jupiter was in attendance. A broad smile crept across his mouth.

The honor of presiding over these meetings rotated through the ranks. Today Neptune lightly tapped the gavel to call the meeting to order. "If you would be kind enough to inform us why we're here, Bacchus, we'll get started." He glanced at the angle of the sun streaming through the open ceiling. "I have a regatta to attend in an hour, so let's dispense with excess formality. Agreed?"

His suit was navy blue, his shirt stark white, his tie—no surprise there—navy blue. No sense of style whatsoever.

The others, equally lacking in style, murmured their agreement.

Bacchus delivered a flamboyant bow. "I deeply regret that I must be the bearer of such ill tidings." Swiftly he summarized Jupiter's machinations in Cupid's Hollow. The empty streets, the failure to ensure no god or goddess might own a parcel of the land the idiot king wanted to develop for himself (though of course Bacchus didn't refer to Jupiter as *idiot king* in front of his peers). The devastation to an entire community because of one god's greed and excess. The reckless behavior, including the difficult-to-explain destruction of half a hotel worth of television sets because of Jupiter's temper tantrum.

A few of the Consortium shifted in their seats. Their inattentiveness to the topic was his cue. He pulled out his cell phone and played the video of Valentine Arciere shooting Cupid's bow in the middle of a school ground crowded with mortal children.

Frowns broke out.

He had them where he wanted them.

"Ladies and gentlemen, I have the solution. Release these good people from their agreement with Jupitropolis. They never would be in this predicament if Jupiter hadn't overlooked the glaringly obvious problem of a goddess not selling her property. He has taken meddling with mortal lives to a dangerous level that risks our whole world being revealed, and we need to put a stop to it." He pointed his finger in a sweeping gesture that encompassed each Consortium member, including himself. "We need to teach him a lesson."

"That sounds reasonable." Neptune rubbed his forehead. "But it will take time to draw up the appropriate paperwork."

Bacchus smiled.

"Forgive me for taking liberties." He withdrew the specially prepared decree from his pocket, untied the silk ribbon binding it, and unrolled the parchment on the marble table before the god of the sea. "And here's a pen. It would be a travesty if I, of all people, made you late for your day of revelry." He winked.

Someone chuckled. Neptune stood and slapped Bacchus companionably on the shoulder. "Good man," he said, bending to put his name to the decree.

Oh, the poetic beauty of it—that Jupiter's own brother should be the first to sign gave Bacchus an exquisite shiver of pleasure.

One by one, the others followed suit (literally—in their boring, stodgy blues and browns).

He'd believed he could pull this off, of course. But some part of him had thought that Jupiter would manage to throw a wrench in the works. He'd actually done it, though. All this time of kowtowing. Pretending to be less than he was. All worth it in the end. And the brilliant part was that he'd have been happy just winning Valentine Arciere's mortal soul. Now he had won so much more.

Because Bacchus had added a clause to the decree. Just a few words, putting the Consortium's seal of approval to a signed contract that had been delivered to him by his favorite courier. Nobody even noticed it.

When the last signature had been placed, he swept the parchment back into his possession.

The doors slammed open, cracking against the walls.

Bacchus laughed long and loud, letting the vestiges of his mortal disguise fall from him. "My dear friend, I wasn't expecting to see you here."

"Randy?" Recognition dawned on the idiot king's face. "Bacchus," he roared.

"How in the name of the gods did you manage to find that summons, dear boy?" Really, he wanted to know. He'd stuffed it into an empty beer bottle and tossed it behind the wastebasket.

Who would look there? *Why* would one look there?

"You're a pig, and I clean up after you constantly. And I recycle." Jupiter shook his head incredulously. Then, wild-eyed, he charged toward the Consortium. He loomed over the startled gods. "Brother," he thundered to Neptune, jabbing a finger toward Bacchus. The tabletop rattled on its pillars, and the seated gods scooted backward, eyeing the massive slab of marble warily. "This man deliberately prevented me from knowing about the meeting. I demand to be a part of any decision that's to be made this day."

Neptune managed to look appropriately regretful despite sneaking a glance at the angle of the sun. The man did have a regatta to attend, after all.

Bacchus giggled hysterically. He couldn't help it. He giggled until tears streamed down his face and he had to wipe them away with his gloriously festive tie.

"My dear boy," he gasped through his merriment. "I do believe you love the girl."

He was rewarded with a befuddled stare that made him laugh all the harder.

When he could draw a proper breath, he brandished the decree before the face of the idiot king. "But love her or not, you're much too late to influence the outcome of today. The matter has been decided. I own—irrevocably, I might add—the soul of Valentine Arciere."

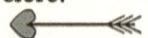

I do believe you love the girl. All the way back to Cupid's Hollow, Vittorio wrestled with the words.

No matter how he argued with himself, he arrived at only one conclusion. He did love Valentine Arciere. He, the king of all gods, renowned for his philandering—his heart bound to one woman. It was unlike him, to be sure, but nothing could remove the truth of it.

He loved her.

And he'd failed her.

She'd lost her soul to Bacchus, distracted by her worry about the audit that Vittorio himself had set in motion.

He'd seen the contract she signed, and it was, as Bacchus said, irrevocable.

For the first time in his life, he didn't know how to proceed.

All he knew was that he loved her and he must go to her.

Holding his breath, he stood on her doorstep and knocked. Please gods she'd deign to talk to him.

The door opened. Gods, she was the most lovely creature he'd ever seen. Those honey-warm eyes… turned as icy as the wind that crept under the collar of his merino jacket. She slammed the door.

He was faster and blocked it with his forearm, remembering the damage done to his foot last time he'd blocked a door open with it. "Please, Valentine."

Her ice melted just a little. Just enough. She relaxed her hold on the door and backed up. Could it be possible that she loved him, too? Even if she had some tidbit of caring in her heart for him, he'd be satisfied with it. Just a crumb.

He didn't even recognize himself anymore. All his surety was gone. His happiness pivoted on whether she returned his feelings—and the only thing he could give her was his apology for having helped her lose her soul. How could any woman accept a man who had done such a thing?

Vittorio cleared his throat. He wanted to take her in his arms and comfort her, but not before he told her the truth. "I fear I bear ill tidings."

She looked askance at him, and he reminded himself not to say things like *ill tidings*. Oh, toss it. He was too set in his ways to worry about sounding old-fashioned.

Her expression went from annoyance to suspicion to curiosity, and finally she opened the door. "You'd better come in so I can shut the door."

Gratefully, he stepped inside the little house that was so unlike his massive stone temple. So homey, so warm, so… Valentine. "Thank you."

She beckoned for him to follow her to the kitchen and busied herself with mugs and a coffeepot. She flashed a bitter glance at him as she handed him a steaming cup. "I don't know how your tidings could be any more ill than anything else you've brought to Cupid's Hollow, frankly."

Something hollow took up residence in the place below his stomach. What a dolt he'd been where she was concerned. Had he no care for the things she cared about? She had built her life in this community. And he had run roughshod over her and it, destroying both for the sake of his ambition.

"For what my apology is worth, I am sorry for what I have done to Cupid's Hollow." He dared to touch the softness of her cheek with his finger. "No business deal is worth hurting you."

Her lashes dipped, drawing his attention down to the fullness of her lips. When she opened her eyes, the hurt in them was like a battering ram to his gut. "When were you going to tell me that if I signed that buy-out agreement, you'd own my soul?"

He steeled himself and drew his hand back from her. "I should have told you the moment I realized you were not mortal. But your transformation rather… distracted me." He gripped the hot mug tightly, deserving to feel the pain searing his palm. "No, that's not—you deserve better, and now I must hurt you again."

"Oh, please. Like you could hurt me." She took a long sip of coffee that must burn her throat, but she didn't even flinch. "All there is between us is a lie. Gram shot us with love arrows. It's not real. So don't get your panties in a twist, okay? I'm fine."

She was a terrible liar. Tears brimmed on her lower lashes. He desired, more than anything he'd ever desired, to take away the pain he had caused. But instead he must wrench the knife harder so that he may tell her the truth.

The hopelessness of ever winning back her heart brought him to his knees on the tiled kitchen floor.

"Oh, get up," she scolded him.

He could not. He opened his mouth and let the ugliness of the truth spill out. About his carelessness. About Bacchus's treachery and his own role in how she'd come to sign the contract. With each word, he could sense her withdrawing from him until any hope of reconciliation seemed beyond reach. His only consolation was that the other property owners would be handsomely reimbursed for their businesses even though the Jupitropolis would not be built. He told her of that, too. He told her everything, because she deserved to know. "And so now he is in possession of your store, and with it, your soul."

He bowed his head. He couldn't look at her. Didn't want her to see the depth of his shame. Couldn't bear to see the grief he knew must be swimming in her eyes.

"My soul?" Disbelief shook her voice. "That's what all those papers were about?"

He nodded. "Your soul belongs to Bacchus."

Her hands were warm against his cheeks.

"Look at me."

So soft, so gentle was her voice. Cautiously he opened his eyes. She was kneeling before him. Instead of devastation, all he saw in her eyes was a burning determination.

"There are laws," she said. "This Bacchus character had no legal right to take my store—or my soul, which I don't believe for a second belongs to anyone—and I'm not going to stand for it. And you're going to help me get them back."

Before he could explain to her how the laws set by the Consortium differed from mortal laws, she buried her hands in his hair and kissed him. Deeply. Hard. The ferocity of her passion made even him almost believe that she indeed was still in possession of her soul—almost.

Door hinges squeaked somewhere in the house.

"Oh, my."

At her grandmother's exclamation, the two drew apart. Valentine blushed attractively. Vittorio suppressed a groan. He didn't understand why the worst possible news had put Valentine in a mind to make love, but he hadn't been about to question it, either.

"Don't mind me." Maria flapped her hand at them. "My ride is here. I'm off to the salon to have my hair set for the gala… and out for tea with friends… and… ah… I'll be away three or four hours. So you two do what comes naturally," she exclaimed brightly, as though happening upon the king of gods ravishing her granddaughter in the kitchen were an everyday occurrence.

Well. Maria *was* of the line of Cupid.

She trundled herself out of the house.

He and Valentine stayed motionless until the front door shut and he heard the sound of the lock turning.

Val got to her feet and tugged his hand.

Had the interruption broken the mood?

She sent him a smoldering look. "Come with me."

He came with her. Though not as many times as she did.

Afterward, with her bedsheets tangled about their hips, she kissed him again and then nestled her head under his chin. Perhaps he should leave well enough alone, but he must know. "Why did you forgive me?" he murmured into her pale, silky hair.

"You respect me enough to tell me the truth." She didn't raise her face, just hugged him more tightly. "You're the first person who's ever done that."

thirteen

THE RESIDENTS OF Cupid's Hollow came out in full force for the Valentine's Day Gala. Nobody seemed to care that Gram wore fur (she'd finally decided on mink), some wore down parkas, and some wore layers of plaid flannel with trapper-style hats. All that mattered on this annual festivity was that the community celebrated one more year—together.

This was Val's town. Her community. This was where she belonged. This was where she'd stay and fight for her store. And for her soul, though she couldn't make herself believe that it had been sold as part of a real estate contract, no matter how earnestly Vittorio tried to convince her of it.

She scanned the throng of revelers for the brightly clad man who'd accompanied Vittorio to the library the ill-fated day she'd broken up with him. The god Bacchus, it seemed, had been disguising himself as an assistant named Randy. She'd like to give him a piece of her mind.

Vittorio pointed toward a booth that was selling alcoholic beverages. The chubby bartender wore the only Hawaiian-print parka she'd ever seen. It wasn't a good look. "There."

Elation coursed through her, and she whooped. "Let's go get him. And let's get a drink."

A hand held her back. Vittorio frowned. "We don't exactly have a plan, and I assure you, a drink poured by Bacchus isn't going to help."

Yeah, okay. "I really need to talk to him. Right now." She

swiftly undid a few buttons and then slipped from his grasp, leaving her lamé jacket dangling from his hand. "And I'm going to have a glass of that wine," she called over her shoulder as she dashed through a smattering of snowflakes that had begun to fall over the revelers. "We're celebrating, silly!"

She dashed through the crowd, laughing each time Vittorio caught up to her, gliding just out of his reach as she danced through the lineup to Bacchus's booth. She leaned her elbows on the counter and brought her fingers up below her chin. She gave the god of revelry her most appreciative smile. "One glass, please… for everyone, and it's on Vittorio!"

As the wine flowed freely, cheers burst out all around her, from everyone except her fabulously handsome boyfriend. She took his face between her hands and kissed him soundly on the mouth. "Now stop glowering. Didn't anyone ever tell you your face could freeze like that?"

Their faces were inches apart. Something about the way he looked into her eyes made her stop. What was she doing? *Did* Bacchus own her soul?

Vittorio draped her coat around her and fastened the buttons. Warmth seeped into her.

"Come with me, amore mio," he whispered.

The words cut through the cheers and the clinking of glasses.

It was as though a spell had been broken. Val shook her head to clear it. "I think that's a good idea."

"Not so fast." Bacchus leaped over the counter. He waved his hand in a circle over his head. "She belongs to me."

The party all around them seemed to fade and withdraw, the voices muted, the colors pale. Val, Vittorio, and Bacchus stood in an oddly silent clearing in the midst of the gala.

"She belongs to no one." Vittorio put his arm protectively around her. But she could tell he didn't believe what he was saying.

Bacchus only laughed and produced a roll of parchment that he dangled in front of the king's face. "Wrong, as usual." From nowhere, he produced a glass of lovely, bubbling wine and held it out to her.

Val felt her hand rise to take it. She stopped herself. Lowered her hand.

"No."

Gaze darting from the glass to her hand and back, Bacchus frowned. He flicked the glass with his finger, and the clear, bell-like tone called to her like a siren. Held it out again. "Here you go, my dear. Take it."

She wanted to. She wanted to *so bad*.

Val clenched her hands into fists and shoved them deep into her pockets. "No."

"This cannot be." The god of revelry tossed the glass over his shoulder and produced another one. "Try this one."

Nothing had ever been this hard to resist. She shook her head. "I don't want to."

His beady eyes narrowed. "Oh, you want to. So why aren't you?"

A furry little tempest of mink and freshly coiffed gray hair erupted from the edge of the protective circle. Gram trotted up, shaking her finger at Bacchus. "Because trickery and deceit are no match for love, you fool."

All three of them gaped at Gram.

"What, you think old people just sit around all day and watch nitwits like this take advantage of the people they love?" She clapped her hands twice. "I summon the Consortium of gods!"

A great whirlwind descended around them, whipping Val's hair. Blades of light cut through the darkness. She shaded her eyes. The wind abated, and one figure after the next stepped down out of the brilliant glare, some looking annoyed, some curious. One old man wearing a navy-blue suit and carrying, of all things, a tall golden trident, strode up to Gram.

"What is the meaning of this, old woman?"

She drew herself up to her full height, which wasn't much. "Neptune. I know what you did. You owe me, and you're going to listen to what I have to say."

Neptune suddenly looked like he'd shrunk three sizes. "I was wrong, Maria. But it cannot be undone."

"Not that," she snapped. "I know you can't bring my child back. What you can do is apologize to *her* child for what you did at the behest of this—this worm." She glared at Bacchus to make it clear which god was the worm she referred to.

Val's stomach sank. Was there no end to what this world of gods had hidden from her? She stepped forward toward Neptune, still feeling the comfort of Vittorio's presence behind her. "Well?"

He met her gaze then looked away.

The air around Gram seemed to tremble. Val thought even the frozen earth below her feet quivered.

Neptune slowly turned back to Val. He tugged at his white beard. "I suppose you deserve the truth."

"Do you think?" Was that her lippy attitude, or was it the marked lack of inhibition she'd been experiencing since Bacchus claimed he owned her soul? Vittorio's squeeze on her shoulder suggested it might be Bacchus's influence.

Bacchus was sidling away. Neptune raised his trident, and the god of revelry sighed theatrically and trudged back to join his peers.

"The capsizing of *Salacia* was not an accident," Neptune confessed.

"I know that." Val, with no warning, tipped backward as though she were drunk. She thought she heard Bacchus titter. Vittorio was there behind her, holding her up. She regained her balance. "And I know why."

Neptune released a weary sigh. "No, child. You don't know everything."

"Do tell." Gram glared at Neptune.

"Do we really need to go into the sordid details?" Bacchus backed up.

Vittorio cleared his throat to catch the attention of Neptune, who snagged the potential escapee on a prong of his trident and propped it up so that Bacchus was dangling with his feet a few inches off the ground. "You were present at the beginning of this matter, and you shall be present at the end of it."

"Let's get on with it," another god grumbled.

Vittorio's touch grew heavier and firmer. Thunder bellowed through the odd grouping of onlookers, shimmering against a dome of night that surrounded them. "I would hear this tale."

Something seemed off to Val. Something more than the fact that she was the progeny of Cupid, surrounded by twenty or thirty purportedly mythological beings.

The golden filaments interconnecting the gods and goddesses were gleaming more and more brightly; none so bright as the one that connected her with Vittorio. And while some threads shone gold and—the only way she could describe it was *true*—others were frayed. Intermittent. As though—

"She has the sight," Bacchus blurted.

An instant snapshot formed before her eyes, like string art she'd seen in her childhood, different colors of threads arranged on a board to make a picture. This one wasn't a picture of an object, it was a picture of intent. She knew with absolute certainty which of the members of the Consortium would use her without qualm and which would stand by her side. There were far more of the former than the latter. She felt trapped by them and suddenly understood far too well why Gram had made her promise not to tell anyone she had the sight.

"Enough," Vittorio roared, forcing the others to back up a step through sheer force of will—combined with the force of the thunder and lightning his fury generated. "How did you know?"

Bacchus pointed at Gram. "I heard it from the loose lips of Maria herself."

Gram looked sick. Not as sick as Val felt. He must have overheard them talking.

Vittorio shoved Val behind him and addressed the others. "You shall not use her for your ends, and you shall not harm her."

Val stepped around him. Everyone except Gram was cowering (Bacchus, still dangling from the trident, managed to cower by drawing himself up into the fetal position). And except Val, of course. Because even without the beautiful shining light between her and Vittorio, she knew to her core that she could trust him with her life. "Thank you, sweetheart. If you don't mind, I have something to say."

She faced Bacchus. "Neptune said you had something to do with my parents' death. I have a feeling it was because of something more than just my mother having the sight—which, in case you're wondering, I'm not going to let you exploit, so don't even ask—so let's have it. Why did *Salacia* really go down that day?"

The god of revelry didn't look too much like he was having a good time. Val wished she had a superpower that was as intimidating as Vittorio's thunder. Or a trident to brandish like Neptune's. But aside from her bow and arrows, all she had was this blazing need to hear the truth. "Tell me," she commanded.

Her voice was soft, but it reverberated through the crowd. Gram nodded approvingly. Gods and goddesses shuffled closer. Bacchus drew a breath deeper than she'd have thought possible. He blew it out. Then he repeated the procedure.

Finally he uncurled himself. "It's not exactly—at least not completely—my f—"

"No excuses," she said. "The truth. Now."

She could sense that nobody really was even breathing. Everyone wanted to hear whatever *sordid* truth Bacchus might reveal.

"Fine." He sighed petulantly. "As the god of revelry, I couldn't just stand by and let your silly little school and the silly little parents' committee throw a dry grad party," he jeered. "Imagine young people everywhere abstaining from the fruit of the vine. And your parents were campaigning for their cause across the country. Who would worship me? I'd be finished."

Once again she needed Vittorio's physical support in order to remain on her feet. "You murdered my parents because they wanted to keep me safe?"

A low thunder rumbled through the collection of gods. It wasn't Vittorio, though.

"That's low." "Swine." "Playing god, eh, Bacchus?"

A titter.

Then Vittorio let loose with his own brand of thunder so loud that Val clapped her hands over her ears until it passed. "We'll leave your punishment for that, and for the mess you made in Valentine Sports—because don't think for a minute I don't know about that—to another time, because there's something more important to deal with tonight. Neptune, as the chair of the last meeting of the Consortium, you bear responsibility here. Proceed, please."

"Ah. Yes." Neptune glanced up at the still-dangling god of revelry. "Can I set him down? He's awfully heavy."

"No." Vittorio crossed his arms.

"Very well. This needs to be quick, then." The god of the sea, who surely could have saved her parents but hadn't, gave Val the most mournful look she'd ever seen. "I'm deeply sorry, my dear."

"Don't call me that." She didn't think she needed to explain why.

"Indeed." He had the grace to look ashamed. "Ms. Arciere, then. While I would like very much to undo what Bacchus has done, the contract we all signed—"

"I didn't sign it," Vittorio shouted.

"*Most* of us signed… must stand. There's nothing we can do to *undo* it."

Gram tottered up, elbowing Bacchus and causing him to sway wildly, to Neptune's dismay. She fixed her huge blue gaze on the god of the sea.

"Nonsense. The terms of the contract that Val was tricked into signing"—she gave Bacchus a swift knock with her elbow that sent him spinning—"stipulates that she signs over her property *and* her soul, a package deal, one not included without the other. Does it not?"

"Yes. A contract term that *most* gods and goddesses would know to avoid at all cost." Neptune's stringy arm was beginning to quiver under the strain of holding up Bacchus's portly form. "Her soul goes with her property."

"But he didn't know, did he, that *my* name is on that deed, too?" Gram pointed to herself smugly. "And he most certainly does not possess *my* soul. I didn't sign anything."

Val's stomach dropped.

"Gram, no."

Bacchus, still spinning, began to cackle. "Two for the price of one! Oh, I just can't lose today."

Neptune conferred with the others. When they finished, he looked positively sick. "I see what you're trying to do, but I'm afraid Bacchus is right, Maria."

A rumbling grew behind Val. The air crackled with electricity. She held up her hand. "No, Vittorio. This is my fight."

She knew what she wanted to say and took a moment to get it straight in her mind. So much was at stake, and this sneaky little man was slippery—and smart. She didn't want him to get away with murder*and* her soul. And now Gram's.

"What is a soul?" Nobody answered her. "Come on. You're gods, people! This should be simple for you."

A hand came up from the edge of the crowd. Its owner wore a winged hat. "Mercury, Ms. Arciere. A soul is the very essence of a person."

That one response set up a chain reaction. "A soul is a person's will." "A person's heart." "A soul is the source of loyalty." And on and on.

Val didn't turn to Vittorio. She already knew she could count on him. No, she turned to the most ill-intending member of the entire gathering.

"Bacchus." She smiled coolly at him. "In any way, have I demonstrated that my essence, my will, my heart, or my loyalty is yours to command?"

"B-but." First confusion then dismay played over his pudgy features.

"You can't have my soul without my property, and you can't have my property without my soul. So I guess you do lose. Because despite all your machinations, I haven't done your bidding even once."

"By gum," Neptune exclaimed. "The girl has a point. What say you?" He swept his trident over the others, sending Bacchus flying in an alarming arc that made everyone in his path scurry to safety.

The god of revelry thumped to the ground with a grunt. He pushed himself up and pointed to her. "No. She's mine, I say! The sight is mine. I'll prove it. Now take your bow and shoot him"—he pointed to Neptune, and then to Mercury and several others—"and him and him, and her!"

Cackling, he watched her expectantly.

"Silence." Neptune pinned him down, a prong of the trident piercing the ground on either side of his neck.

Something in her felt a nearly undeniable urge to respond to his command; but if she gave in to it, she'd be the one willingly signing over her soul. This moment would decide the matter once and for all. She would have no recourse.

Difficult as it was, Val crossed her arms and raised her eyebrow.

The trident dug in deep enough to make its prisoner squirm. Neptune looked less than pleased. "I'd say that settles, it, but this is for the Consortium to decide. Does Valentine Arciere have possession of her soul as you, the Consortium of gods, have defined it or not?"

Though many looked uncomfortable—the ones whom Val knew without doubt would *not* have her back—one god nodded, and another joined. Even the ones the sight told her were filled with ill intent cast their votes for her. Only Bacchus abstained.

"Very well. The contract in question is null and void." Neptune flipped his trident and pounded its staff on the ground in a pronouncement. "And, I might add, Maria is of course exempt as well… stubborn old goat that she is," he added under his breath.

A whoosh filled the air, and the other gods were swept away on the wind. She caught the flash of taillights trailing up into the sky like red fireflies. The dome that had shielded them from the gala shimmered and then faded.

Val watched as the taillights twinkled and then disappeared. "That was… quick."

Vittorio shrugged. "Neptune is in the middle of a regatta."

Well, that made a ton of sense.

Gram tugged her sleeve. "We have business still to settle, I think."

Marching toward them at the head of a phalanx of Cupid's Hollow former Main Street business owners, John Jones wore a determined expression.

The townspeople came to a halt before her. People she'd worked with all her life, celebrated with, grieved with, grown up with. The phalanx dissolved, and she was surrounded by excited chatter.

"We knew you'd pull through," John said gruffly, pulling her into a quick hug. "Much longer, we'd have been collecting employment insurance."

Everyone was patting her head and thumping her back as though she'd done something heroic.

Her hat had slipped down over her eyes, and she pushed it up and gazed at the others. So much joy. So much relief.

They think that because I'm with Vittorio, I'm going to sell out.

Since the day her shop had been broken in to and someone had nailed the Jupitropolis buy-out contract to her wall, she'd known how much all of them were hurting for money. Because of her. And she'd managed to block that out of her mind. Well, she couldn't anymore, because what affected them affected her. She may be a goddess, with who knew what kind of obligations to the world of deity, but her heart knew she had to be accountable to the people of Cupid's Hollow first.

She sought his hand with hers, and he gave it a gentle squeeze.

She trusted him. She trusted him with her life.

Wouldn't it be best for everyone if she sold the store to him?

Fireworks erupted all around them, great booms and flashes, a spectacle to accompany celebration. Everyone cheered.

Selling her store to Vittorio literally meant selling her soul.

"I... can't."

Why was she so selfish?

Even Gram looked shocked.

John's joyful expression shattered into disbelief.

A burst of fireworks crackled around them like strobe lights. People were starting to grumble, and she half expected some of the plaid flannel crowd to brandish flaming torches.

Val's throat ached from holding back her sobs.

"I understand why you cannot say yes, amore mio," Vittorio murmured. "Let me speak to them."

She nodded and stepped back, wondering how even the king of gods could possibly salvage any of this situation.

His voice rang over the *bang* and *crack* of the exploding fireworks. "People of Cupid's Hollow, as the owner of Jupitropolis, I cannot in good conscience watch this town become divided, watch you good people face financial disaster, because of my store." He was so earnest. She knew he meant every word he said, and the townspeople gravitated toward him, not needing any special powers to understand he really cared about them. "Also as the owner of Jupitropolis, I have made the decision that I will pay out all property owners immediately, regardless of the contract terms."

That was so, so much more than the Consortium had decreed he should do.

The stunned silence lasted no more than a few seconds. Whooping and hollering ensued. The glitter of joyous tears trickled down more than a few faces, reflecting in the continuous barrage of light from the fireworks. In the pauses between explosions, the network of gold filaments clothed the community in a garment of love and harmony so beautiful she couldn't suppress her tears any longer.

Vittorio held up his hands. "And if one day I do build one of my stores in your community, each of you is guaranteed a job, full medical and dental benefits, and a robust retirement plan."

Val was the worst person ever. Why couldn't she make herself say yes?

SUSAN LOHRER

"In addition, I'll be improving the benefit plans of all employees in all of my stores."

She couldn't take this any longer. She didn't deserve Vittorio, and she didn't deserve her friends and neighbors. Now that she knew without doubt what the right thing was, why couldn't she just *do* it?

"I'm so sorry. Everybody, I'm just... I'm sorry." She whirled and ran to her car.

fourteen

"VAL." *BOOM, BOOM, boom.* "Valentine, open the door."

Groggy after a long night filled with restless dreams and regret, Val pulled the pillow harder around her ears. She didn't want to face anyone. Not even Deb, who seemed intent on bashing her bedroom door down. "Go away."

The doorknob turned. The door squeaked. Deb bulldozed right in and swiped the pillow. "You need to see this."

Val sent her the most baleful glower she could muster. She pulled the sheets over her head. "I don't feel well. I may be coming down with something." Something like a terminal case of guilt.

"Val!" Deb laughed.

Wait. Val peeked out. "Why are you so happy?"

"I'm not telling." She did a little dance. "All I'll say is that Maria and I had a long chat, and you and I are friends, and that's that."

"By any chance did anybody shoot you with an arrow recently?" If Gram was playing with Cupid's bow again, Val would have to lock the darned thing up in a safe deposit box.

"I think I'd have noticed." Deb gave her a look that said *you've lost your mind but I like you anyhow*, and she tossed her a pair of jeans. "You need to get up and face the day. Get dressed. You're coming for a little drive. I promise it'll be worth it."

Val pushed the covers aside, more than a little relived

that her best friend no longer hated her. "Can you just tell me? Because my shop is destroyed, I'm being audited, and I singlehandedly prevented Cupid's Hollow from getting its Jupitropolis. I really don't know if I *can* face the day."

"Do I need to stand here and make sure you get dressed? Because if I have to, I will."

That didn't sound like an idle threat. It would be less trouble to go with Deb than to keep arguing with her—or being forcibly hauled out of bed and dressed by Deb.

Val huffed. "Give me five minutes."

"That's more like it."

She got dressed, made a trip to the bathroom, and pulled a comb through her hair. No amount of makeup would have disguised the rough night she'd had, so she didn't bother with any. When she climbed into Deb's car, Gram was already in the backseat, grinning like a loon. But she refused to tell Val what was going on. "You have to see it with your own eyes, child," she insisted as they pulled away from the curb.

"Okay," Deb announced as they approached Main Street. "Close your eyes."

The boarded-up window of Valentine Sports was the last thing she wanted to see this morning. "Already done."

"Oh, Valentine," Gram gasped. "It's magnificent."

Val's eyes popped open. The entire four-block-long stretch of Main Street was… gone. Overnight. Disappeared.

In its place stood a towering edifice bearing a massive, brightly lit sign.

Jupitropolis.

Not even the king of gods could erect such a huge building in one night. Could he?

Cars lined both sides of the street, so Deb double-parked. "Come. This isn't the surprise. You need to see what's inside."

Stunned, her head swiveling as though she were a tourist, Val let Deb lead her through the bank of glass doors into a milling throng of shoppers and Jupitropolis employees. She knew every one of them, had known them all her life.

How could nobody but her think this was impossible?

Gram clapped her hands. "That's my boy," she cheered.

Front and center in the megastore was Valentine Sports. The racks had been stood up, the merchandise restored to its displays. The glass had been replaced in the big display window.

Val pressed her fingers over her mouth.

"So, what do you think?" Vittorio's voice was the best thing she'd ever heard. She turned to him.

"You did this. All that stuff about *if* you build a store in Cupid's Hollow—you had this planned all the time."

"Since last night, yes," he admitted. "I find your refusal to compromise your convictions quite… attractive." He gave her a slow smile full of promise. "Despite what you think, you care about the people of Cupid's Hollow more than you care about yourself. You can't be happy if they're in need. And so how could I not find a way to make you happy? Amore mio, how could I not woo you?"

He pulled her into his arms and kissed her soundly, to a chorus of cheers and a few wolf whistles.

Her face heated, but she let her mouth linger on his a little longer before she pulled away. She didn't deserve any of this, but somehow it was hers. Her shop, her community, Gram… and the man she held in her arms, her heart's desire.

For a moment she let herself remember that if not for Gram shooting her with a love arrow—and her shooting Vittorio under the table at the restaurant—she might not feel that way about him at all. But only for a moment. Everything he had done since she met him, everything he'd said, came from a place of honesty and respect. He'd literally risked his life—the life of a god—to ensure her safe transformation to her goddess form. He didn't have to do any of that. Even without magic influencing her, she loved the person he was.

"Vittorio, I—thank you. Thank you so much."

An insistent tapping on her shoulder made her look at Gram, who blinked up at her. "You know what, Val, I forgot to tell you something."

Her heart jerked just a little bit inside her ribs. She turned in the circle of Vittorio's arms. "Forgot to tell me what, Gram?"

Gram looked around them. Val did, too. She had a feeling that whatever Gram was about to say would be best said without mortal ears nearby. And they were in luck—despite the heavy shopper traffic, they were relatively isolated at the moment. Deb had wandered off toward the menswear department for some reason and was inspecting the spring collection of Hawaiian print shirts Val would have to have a talk with her—or perhaps employ a platinum arrow if it came to it.

But that could wait.

She returned her attention back to Gram, who was wearing an unusually smug expression, even for her.

"I took an inventory of the arrows the other day. The one I shot you with the day you met Vittorio"—she beamed with satisfaction—"it was a hate arrow."

"What… does that mean?" She'd seen how fast the arrows affected others. Was their effect on a goddess slower-acting? Would her feelings for Vittorio fade? And why was Gram so pleased about it?

"It means a great deal, child." Gram patted her arm. "It means your love for Vittorio is so strong, so real, so true, even the strongest magic of the gods cannot undermine it."

Vittorio, his arm still around Val's shoulders, dropped a kiss on Gram's cheek. It made her giggle like a young girl. Then he nuzzled Val. "Come. There is one more thing."

He guided her to the door of Valentine Sports and gestured for her to open the door.

Wondering at his uncharacteristic lack of chivalry, Val pushed the glass door inward. A tinkling sound greeted her, and she looked up.

There was her bell. And tied with a red ribbon to the clapper was a diamond ring fit for a goddess.

Vittorio reached up and pulled the end of the ribbon. The ring dropped into his hand, and he reached for hers.

"Amore mio." His voice was thick with emotion. A trick of light and shadow there on the threshold of the store allowed her to see the thread of light that connected the two of them, and it made Vittorio and her seem to glow. Or maybe the glow was caused by the strength of her love for him. He dropped to one knee and offered the ring. "May I?"

She couldn't find her voice, so she nodded. The relief that flooded his face was so intense, she laughed aloud.

Vittorio jumped to his feet and wrapped his arms around her in a hug so tight, she could barely breathe. "I wasn't sure you'd say yes."

"Well, I do." After enjoying the hug most thoroughly, she realized he was still holding the ring. So she pried open his hand and slid her finger through the slim band of gold.

It fit perfectly.

Connect

E-mail Susan at susan@susanlohrer.com

Get e-mail alerts (once or twice a year) about Susan's new releases by signing up for her newsletter at www.susanlohrer.com/p/newsletter.html

Find Susan on Facebook
https://www.facebook.com/Author.Susan.Lohrer

Other Books by Susan Lohrer

Rocky Road (contemporary romance)

Over the Edge (contemporary romance)

Eagle Magus (fantasy romance, book 1 of Magus series)

Coming soon:

The Harrington series (small-town contemporary romance)

Wooing Bacchus (contemporary fantasy romance; book 2 of the Wooing the Gods series)

Wooing Mercury (contemporary fantasy romance; book 3 of the Wooing the Gods series)

Wolf Magus (fantasy romance; book 2 of Magus series)

Last Magus (fantasy romance; book 3 of Magus series)

A Taste of Rocky Road:

Wouldn't someone who really wanted to get married be a little more careful than this? Not that Ancy doubted Mark's intentions. He was The One. And she wouldn't nag him about it.

Honestly though, severing most of the nerves in his hand should've been enough for one week—but no! He had to go and whop himself on the head too. It wasn't like Mark to be this accident-prone, and he'd been getting worse over the last few months. Working too hard so he'd be a good provider, no doubt. That's just the kind of guy he was. She smiled, visualizing him in a black tux.

Focusing on her impending nuptials usually distracted her from thinking about whether she'd make department head. And lately, her impending groom had been more than enough distraction.

She checked the temperature of the paraffin tub. "This'll feel a little hot, but it'll help with flexibility." He grimaced as she dipped his right hand into the warm wax. Then he gave her bum a squeeze with the left one. "Quit it before someone sees us."

Since he wasn't dragging his feet—that much seemed obvious—why couldn't he stay in one piece long enough to put some professional distance between them?

"Mark, you've dropped a wall on your head, nailed your foot to the floor, and dislocated your shoulder. Are you trying to get out of our wedding?"

Whoops.

She bit her lip and glanced over her shoulder. Outpatient Physical Therapy was crowded in the afternoon. The last thing she needed was for someone to overhear her in a lover's spat… with her patient. That would not only prevent her promotion to department head, it would end her career. Instantly. Working quickly, she covered the warm wax with a plastic bag, then slipped a padded mitten over the whole thing to lock in the heat.

If only there were a simple way to get around the patient-therapist dating taboo. But because her specialty was post-traumatic hand rehabilitation, she was the therapist most qualified to care for Mark's injuries—so she and Mark were forced into secrecy until he regained the use of his hand. "Well, couldn't you try to be just a little more careful?" She kept her voice to a low hiss. "At this rate, I'll be ninety by the time we even set the date."

"Aw Ancy, a few more weeks and this thing will be as good as new." He grinned and held up his thickly swaddled hand.

Yeah, right. She'd treated her share of injuries. This one was far from pretty, even though she hadn't seen it until after the surgery. His poor body. "Please just be more careful. I want to wear my ring on my finger, not on my necklace where no one can see it." She displayed her perfectly healthy left hand, its third finger perfectly naked. Did Mark have any idea how hard it was on her to keep this a secret? And not just from the department—from Jen, her best friend in the whole world.

Though she was the one best qualified to treat Mark, Jen—perky, sexy Jen—could have treated his injuries. But then Jen and Mark—not that she didn't trust him—but why create temptation by throwing her beefcake fiancé into the capable arms of her best friend? Besides, every difficult PT case brought her another step closer to becoming department head. She couldn't risk losing that kind of security, not when she almost had it in her grasp.

"Promise me you'll be careful."

"You worry too much." He looked so hot when he gave her that wink that said she could count on him no matter what.

"Mark, I'm serious." She added a stern, professional note to her voice as Doris Ridgewood, the department head—who was due for retirement any second—passed by. "You have to take some time off work to rest. If you don't, you'll never regain full use of your hand."

Doris nodded approvingly and continued on her way.

Mark leaned close. "It's kind of exciting, don't you think, Ance?"

"What is?" She checked her watch. Almost time to unwrap the hand and work on scar mobility.

"Knowing you'll be mine to have and to hold." He waggled his dark brows meaningfully. "This hand is going to make a full recovery, and you know what I'm gonna do with it."

She could feel the blood rushing from her extremities, and probably from a few vital organs, straight to her face.

Jen, between patients, was walking past. Had she overheard Mark's titanically not-suitable-for-work innuendo? She slowed. Cocked her head. Pivoted on her heels. Ancy's promotion slithered down to the pit of her belly as Jen marched up to her and pulled her aside, a thunderstorm brewing in her eyes. "Is this guy giving you a hard time?"

Fresh guilt welled up inside Ancy, and she was sure her cheeks were as red as if Jen had targeted her with a laser pointer. Jen didn't have a clue, and it made Ancy feel like a big, fat liar.

"I um, got something in my eye." Jen shot her a strange look. But it was the only thing Ancy could think of on such short notice. She turned away and pretended to wipe at her face. When she looked again, Jen was with another patient. Ancy had never kept a secret from her best friend before, and she was starting to hate the way it made her feel.

Maybe she should tell Jen and just get this whole thing off her shoulders. But then Jen would be obligated to tell Doris, and Ancy wouldn't blame her if she did. And she'd lose her job. Her watch's second hand swept up to the 12.

Back to Mark.

The mitten, the bag, and the wax came off, and she began to manipulate his hand through range-of-motion exercises, bending and stretching all his fingers, careful not to apply too much pressure to the still-healing surgery scars. His hands were muscular. Strong hands, dependable hands. The hands of a man who would stand by her through whatever life threw at them. And he wouldn't leave her the way Steve had. The way her father had left her family.

"Nice technique, Ancy." Doris's voice behind her shoulder made her flinch. The woman didn't approach like a normal person, she appeared. Ancy had never once heard her coming. "Young man," Doris said, skimming over the floor and coming to stand beside Ancy, "our Miss Robertson is highly qualified in her specialty. She's one of the best."

Wow. It wasn't every day Doris handed out a compliment like that. Could it reflect an intention to recommend Ancy for the promotion?

"Of course, Fidelity General Hospital is soon to be blessed with a second, equally qualified therapist. He's one of our alumni. Your case might prove especially interesting to him." She glided away, and Ancy pictured Doris as a young, heavy-browed girl balancing a book on her head.

Her mind was racing. "Mark, do you realize what this means? It's the answer to our problems." Because an equally qualified therapist who didn't have her seniority could take over Mark's case without threatening her promotion. Then the bit about the alumnus sank in.

"Ouch, let go!" Mark's face contorted.

Ancy loosened her grip immediately and banished the unsettling thought from her mind. "I'm sorry." She returned to her work on his hand and whispered, "You can switch to the new therapist, and we can come out in the open."

She pulled the curtain halfway around the bench for a little more privacy before starting to work on Mark's other injuries. These weren't as serious as the one to his hand, and while she concentrated on deltoidius, trapezius, and rhomboideus major and minor, she couldn't help but notice Mark's build on a more superficial level, which was part of the reason she'd pulled the curtain. Half the staff would be drooling over him if they saw his bare chest.

As it was, all she could manage to say to him when she finished the examination was, "Looks good."

The curtain behind her swished open, and the scent of Obsession for Men filled her mind with images from the past.

Steven Stone. Steve and her, training together, working together. Steve, the only guy who'd ever made an effort to understand her autistic brother and had never made fun of him. Steve and her, in his fossil fuel–burning Mustang….

Steve… the second and last man who'd walked out of her life. A wall slammed down in her heart.

It couldn't be him. She made herself turn around. Her arm brushed the paraffin tub, and liquid wax sloshed over the sides. A distant splash marked its landing on the floor.

Her heart did that funny flipping thing that made her breath catch in her throat.

It was him.

A Taste of Over the Edge:

Kat shifted her wrists in the steel handcuffs. Rough, ancient bark pressed against her cheek, and the damp air intensified the resinous tang of the virgin forest. She'd been here since dawn—long enough to be on a first-name basis with Harvey, the Douglas fir. Which, if she let herself consider for more than a minute at a time, was kind of a weird development for a grown woman who had a respectable career. She'd consider it in more depth later. Right now she had enough on her mind.

A gust of coastal wind snatched her hat, and chilly rain plastered her hair to her scalp and trickled down her neck, making her teeth chatter. Nearby, a group of men wielded wrenches on a logging machine that refused to start. One of her students, the school board superintendent's son, retrieved the hat and plopped it back on Kat's head.

"Don't worry," he whispered, "they're not going to get that machine going anytime soon."

Alarm nibbled the back of her mind like a classroom gerbil gnawing a toilet paper tube. "There'd better not be a reason you know that."

He laughed. "I'm just saying." Then, calling to his friends, he trotted off.

Kat wondered whether she'd still have her job at the end of the day.

The superintendent had made it clear she'd lose it in a blink if the kids did anything more than show up, and Kat had made them promise not to chain themselves to any trees. So far, all they'd done was text the protest's breaking news to their friends… unless they'd messed with the equipment before she got here this morning. The thought made her stomach feel like she'd eaten fir needles for lunch. She stared up into the dense boughs radiating from Harvey's trunk high above her.

"You don't think the kids wrecked that machine, do you, Harv? I mean, they know my career is at stake here." Harvey only sighed in the wind, branches waving toward the broken-down machine. Yeah, it had Kat a little worried, too.

She flexed her shoulders, stiff from the hours she'd spent shackled to the tree. She wasn't against logging; she lived in a wood-frame house and used reams of paper. What school principal didn't? And the logging industry in Mills Creek fed a lot of families.

In the last few hours, she'd had a chance to reevaluate her reasons for chaining herself to this tree. This was about so much more than the environment. It was about standing up for someone who couldn't stand up for herself. Or in Harvey's case, himself. It was about choices that had been taken away from her. It was about the fact that sometimes, no matter how wrong you were, you couldn't undo what you'd done.

Her goal wasn't to stop the logging, this community's lifeblood. It was to protect something beautiful and precious. If she could win this one small battle, do this one small good deed, save just this one tree, maybe it would somehow make amends in her heart for what she'd let happen to her family.

A Jeep rattled up the steep gravel road and pulled off on the landing, followed a few seconds later by a police car. The sun chose that moment to peek through the saturated clouds scudding across the sky as though to mock Kat, and she clenched her jaw.

A man exited the passenger door of the Jeep. His footsteps scuffed on the dirt road. Craning her neck, she peered through slanting late-afternoon shadows, making out only his easy gait and the set of his broad shoulders. Had they brought in a negotiator? He leaned into the police car for a minute, then stood, head down, hands on his hips, like a man bearing a heavy burden.

She almost felt sorry for the guy. She might look like a waterlogged rat at the moment, but he had no idea what he was up against. A tiny smirk crept over her mouth.

Now that this block of forest had been opened up to clear-cut logging, Harvey would have to watch while his family was torn away, one by one. She knew how he felt because the same thing had happened to her, until she had just one family member left. And she and Lacey weren't even on speaking terms at the moment.

She dug her fingers into Harvey's sturdy bark. "What am I doing talking to trees instead of making things right between Lacey and me?"

Soft footfalls on the carpet of needles behind her.

She straightened as much as she could. The chain connecting the two sets of handcuffs slipped and pulled her down with it until she had to slump against the tree trunk.

"Kat, what are you doing?" He sounded as exhausted as she felt. Sounded… disturbingly familiar.

That voice. Evan. Here? Memories grabbed her heart and sliced through it like the blade of the nearby feller buncher waiting to chop the young trees from their roots—if the loggers could get it running again. She strained her eyes to the left, looking without turning her head.

Evan was watching her, jaw clenched, rainwater slicking his blond hair.

She blinked the water from her eyes.

He was still there.

Not a gorgeous hallucination. A gorgeous reality. Her pulse whumped in her ears.

What was she doing? That was easy—she was running away from her failure to keep her family together. But what was Evan doing?

A Taste of Eagle Magus:

Loyalty had raised Varick Garth to leader of his winged strike unit, it had stood by his side while comrades died at the hands of the Maguses, and it had fallen with his soul when he allowed his wings to be severed for the sake of his people. He steeled himself against the exhaustion that plagued him. Despite the weeks that had passed since the wounds on his back finally healed, each night the sound of his own screams wrenched him awake as flesh parted from flesh. His loyalty. His choice.

Now, as Commander Einar raised his wings and spoke to the gathered units of the strike force, his graying feathers glinting silver against patches of late-winter snow in the fading light, Varick pushed back his shoulders, trying not to let the stretch of scar tissue remind him that of all the Wings, none but him had stepped forward to sacrifice what he had for the sake of his people. The mingled scents of sweat and preening oil, the scents that had defined his life for thirty years and even brought comfort to him, now seemed cloying. He forced himself to breathe deeply of what he had lost. Loyalty to his strike unit, to the strike force, and what the Wings stood for was all he had left.

"It is our responsibility to all the peoples of this land." The commander's voice rolled over the ranks of fighters, singling him out. "For the sake of the winged and the ground-walkers alike, the Veil between this world and the next must be closed forever." His gaze fell on Varick, as he had known it would. "Will you accept this task?"

The words weighed heavy on his shoulders. Even now, all rested on his decision. A death sentence whether he succeeded or failed. He could decline, and lots would be drawn. Someone else would be chosen. But to live, and not to fly… that was worse than death anyway. He raised his fist to his chest. "I will."

Einar drew back his wings. "It has been proclaimed."

"So shall it be done," the men responded as one. Fists against leather-clad chests thumped through the ranks like the sound of beating wings.

As the echo of their voices faded and some lifted off to fly to the barracks while others walked in a show of deference for their brother who had given up what they would not, some casting him pitying glances and others unable to meet his eyes at all, the weight of the impossible encased Varick's heart. His wounds had taken so long to heal that little time remained to win the loyalty of a Magus before the Veil rose. Providing he could find a Magus.

About the Author

Susan Lohrer is a Canadian romance author. When she's in a humorous mood she writes funny contemporary romance. When she's in a weird mood she writes fantasy romance. She loves dogs and has way too many aquariums. Her website is www.susanlohrer.com.